I0770791

Echoes of Betrayal

Moira Ashe

Copyright © 2025 Moira Ashe.

All rights reserved. No part of this publication may be reproduced, distributed, or transmitted in any form or by any means, including photocopying, recording, or other electronic or mechanical methods, without the prior written permission of the publisher, except in the case of brief quotations embodied in critical reviews and certain other noncommercial uses permitted by copyright law. For permission requests, write to the author at the website below.

ISBN: 978-1-968712-00-6 (Paperback)

ISBN: 978-1-968712-01-3 (E-Book)

Any references to historical events, real people, or real places are used fictitiously. Names, characters, and places are products of the author's imagination. No identification with actual persons (living or deceased), places, buildings, and products is intended or should be inferred.

Cover design by PJ Thorn, The Smoke Shed (thesmokeshed21@gmail.com).

First printing edition 2025.

www.moiraashe.com

This book contains sexually explicit content and sensitive subjects such as violence and sexual abuse. It is not intended for readers under 18.

MOIRA ASHE

PROLOGUE

The full moon hung overhead, casting an eerie glow on the forest floor as a shovel tore into the earth again and again. Dirt flew over his shoulder in steady rhythm, the pile beside him growing larger with every heave. Blisters burned his palms and sweat soaked through his shirt, but he didn't stop – he couldn't stop. Two days of digging and the hole was just about deep enough.

An hour later, he dragged a heavy, wrapped shape towards the hole. With a grunt, he rolled it in. The weight landed with a thud just as the nearby lantern flickered. He paused, glancing around, eyes scanning the dark beyond the light's reach. Nothing.

When he had finally filled the hole, he dropped onto a fallen log, chest heaving. The forest was quiet, almost unnervingly so. Then he heard it: crunching leaves and snapping twigs. He shot up, struggling to hear over his own heartbeat in his ears. He searched the tree line and though the moon was full and the lantern was bright, the shadows still seemed to stretch a little too far.

A chill ran up his spine. He quickly grabbed the lantern and hurried back to his truck. Slamming the door, he turned the key, the ignition roaring to life and headlights illuminating the night. Looking up, he saw her.

A woman stood just beyond the beams, pale and still.

His breath hitched as he quickly looked from the woman to the woods and back. She was gone. He didn't wait; he drove off, keeping his eyes forward, hoping to leave the woman – and the past – behind him.

PART I

CHAPTER 1

Alyssa Stanton inched her way towards the trees, illuminated only by moonlight. *Breathtaking*, she thought to herself. The full moon hung high above the treetops, casting shadows far across the dewy grass.

Leaves crinkled somewhere in the near distance. Losing her nerve, she turned around and briskly walked towards a dimly lit brick house. While she knew it was likely some forest creature, she couldn't shake the slight fear still crawling on her skin.

Making her way up the steps to the white porch, she paused, glancing around. She took in the scenery - pots filled with various herbs and flowers, two rocking chairs, wind chimes that were now deathly still, and crystal suncatchers that sparkled in the moonlight. She smiled softly. *Home*, she thought. Her hands brushed the lavender posted at the front door as if it were a soldier standing guard. Opening the door, she was greeted by the sight of her husband, Drew, quietly watching a sports game on their living room TV.

He turned his head upon hearing the door open. "Back already?"

She sighed and plopped on the sofa next to him, propping her feet up on his lap. "I couldn't go past the tree line. I feel a presence there, like it's calling to me, trying to pull me deeper into the woods. It's just...I lose my nerve when it's time to take that first step into the trees."

"Maybe you should have brought a flashlight?" He offered with a slight smirk on his face.

Alyssa rolled her eyes at him. "It's not *just* the dark. It's something so familiar, yet so different. I *know* something is in there, but I don't know how I know it. Or even what it is."

"Are you sure you don't want me to come with you?" he pressed.

"It's something I have to do alone. I can't explain it. You know this. But thank you." She leaned over to lightly kiss him on the cheek. "Now, can we please watch something better than this?"

"Seriously?" He rolled his eyes. "You were supposed to be in the woods finding...whatever it is you're looking for...but now that you're back, I can't enjoy a football game?"

"Fine, fine," she said readjusting to now lay on the sofa, her feet still across his lap. She stared up at the ceiling, thinking of the familiar pull she felt outside just minutes ago. *Next time*, she thought. *Next time I'm going to do it*. Her wild imagination took over as she thought of hideous beasts lurking in the woods, just waiting for her to step into their territory and rip her to shreds. She mentally shook her head to clear those images out of her mind. *I will find out what's been calling me.*

That night, Alyssa's dreams were filled with whispers. She found herself standing at the edge of the forest again, but this time, the trees seemed to bend toward her, their branches reaching out like welcoming arms. A soft, melodic humming drifted through the air, carrying with it the scent of rain-soaked earth and something else—something sweet and familiar that she couldn't quite place.

She opened her eyes and glanced at the clock. 3:33 in the morning. She quietly grumbled at waking up. Getting out of bed, she walked to the window and pulled back the curtain, glancing out towards the woods, feeling that familiar pull in her chest. Something seemed off.

There was a light in the distance. A bobbing light that almost looked like a lantern being carried into their forest. But why? Slight fear gripped her heart - fear of the unknown in the distance. She took a step back, bumping into her jewelry armoire, one of the doors opening. A small clank sounded as something fell out.

"You alright?" Drew muttered from the bed.

"Sorry," she whispered back. "I can't sleep." A small fib, but she didn't want to worry him over the light or worse, have him wake up and go investigate. Drew mumbled something unintelligible and turned over, promptly falling back asleep. So much for worrying that he'd check it out. She looked outside again, but the light was gone.

She bent down to pick up what had fallen. It was a necklace that Drew had given her shortly after they had gotten engaged. Rubbing the familiar design, she slightly calmed down, her mind still on the strange light. She was almost positive it wasn't a person, but what else could it be? It was way too big to be a firefly. Maybe it was a will-o'-the-wisp, a small ghostly light seen at night in the woods. *Yeah, that's what it was. Definitely*, she thought to herself, rolling her eyes. She placed the necklace on her nightstand and got into bed.

As she settled back under the covers, the mysterious glow of the light illuminated her mind. Squeezing her eyes shut even tighter did no good. She willed the images to fade and allow her to fall back asleep, but even as sleep slowly enveloped her, the images remained.

Her dreams were filled with floating lights, dark, moonlit trees, and the peaceful chorus of cicadas.

She opened her eyes again, becoming frustrated with her lack of sleep. Thoroughly irritated, she got dressed and decided to go find the disappearing light. She grabbed her phone and paused, deciding to put on the necklace that fell. Snatching her shoes off the floor, she walked out of the bedroom, quietly shutting the door behind her.

Determined to uncover the mystery, she firmly walked towards the woods, forgetting her apprehension of a few hours ago. Arriving at the tree line and turning on her phone's flashlight, she didn't hesitate.

The moment she stepped into the trees, the world started to transform. The scenery before her seemed to melt and meld into something completely different. The soft glow of sunrise shone through the treetops, illuminating the dew and spiderwebs throughout, though she was positive it was dark when she entered. She walked deeper, now unafraid of the unknown in front of her.

She heard a faint noise in the distance. Not an animal, not the wind, but something...human? It almost sounded like humming. She ventured deeper, trying to follow the sound, but the further she went, the more the sound surrounded her. The tone seemed feminine; a soft, melodic sound that was both foreboding and calming.

Placing her hand on a tree, she admired the scenery laid out in front of her. Briars snarled around trees, their leaves hanging listlessly under the weight of the dew, spiderwebs covered in crystal droplets shining in the rising sunlight, and that humming that filled her ears - a humming that she could somehow feel in her soul.

She felt like knew the source of the sound deep inside, but couldn't place it. Remembering she came here looking for the orb of light, she glanced around. The sun shone through the trees, blinding her with a bright blue light.

Wait, a blue light? She put her hands over her brow, trying to block out some of the light while straining to see the source. Her eyes hurt, causing her to look away, leaving her in a state of temporary blindness. As she regained her vision, she looked back to see the light dimming and elongating. "What the hell?" she whispered to herself.

The humming was slowly growing louder. She stood mesmerized at the sight before her, never seeing anything like it in her 25 years.

The light began to take on an almost human-sized shape. The humming was now at a deafening volume. She put her hands over her ears and shut her eyes.

Opening them once more, she found herself in bed, covered in sweat. She sighed. It was just a dream. She grabbed some water, checked the clock - 4:43 a.m. - and rolled over, hoping for some restful sleep this time. She didn't even notice the pendant still hanging from her throat.

CHAPTER 2

T he yellow rays of the sun filtered through the curtains, casting a muted light over Alyssa's face. She cracked open her eyes and groaned. *Five more minutes*, she thought as she rolled over away from the sun's too bright rays.

It had been a month since her last attempt at venturing into the woods. A month since that strange dream she didn't dare mention to Drew. The realization of tonight's moon phase hit her and jump-started her brain. Tonight was the night. The full moon. She was going to finally step foot in there and find that light.

After the dream, she had been inside the woods during the day, but felt and saw nothing. She watched out of the window almost every night, but never saw the light again. She ventured to the tree line during different moon phases, but again didn't feel the same pull. Of course, at night she was too timid to step foot into the woods, but she never felt the calling then, either – only on the full moon.

She silently made her plan as Drew slept next to her. The woods would be illuminated enough by the moonlight to where she shouldn't have an issue with sight, but she planned to bring a flashlight and her phone. Once she gets past the first step, walking deeper should be easy. Determined, she resolved to conquer her fears and do it for real this time.

Sighing, she rolled out of bed, careful not to disturb her husband. Neither were a morning person, but him even less so. She quietly walked out of the room and closed the door behind her. Stomach rumbling, she briefly pondered breakfast then decided on her favorite – pancakes. Taking the easy way out, she grabbed the box of mix and began cooking.

The smell of food must have woken Drew. He fumbled out of the bedroom into the kitchen, sitting down on a barstool across from Alyssa's turned back. "Morning," he grumbled, clearly wishing he was still in bed.

"Hi," she said a little too brightly. "Makin' pancakes. Want some?" She turned and held a plate out, which he accepted, expressing his gratitude. "Tonight's the full moon again. I'm going to do it this time."

"You said that last month," he said, mouth full of pancakes.

"I mean it this time! I've got to know what this feeling is. I've got to know why only at night? Why only during the full moon? Seriously, it doesn't make any sense."

"Ever thought that maybe you're just wanting something exciting to happen? I mean, there's nothing ever going on out here."

"You calling me crazy? Or just don't believe me anymore?"

"No, no I believe you," he quickly backtracked. "It's just that you've been at this for months and haven't gotten anywhere."

"Well, I ignored it for a while and then I've only tried venturing in twice. You know how my nerves get the better of me." She gave a small laugh, almost as if she was trying to convince herself of something. She took a bite out of a finished pancake while waiting for the one in the pan to brown, unable to resist anymore.

"What if it's just your mind playing tricks on you?" he said through bites, clearly more interested in the pancakes than yet another conversation about the forest and her ridiculous pulls towards it. "You know our brains can play weird games."

"Last time..." she paused biting her lip, unsure if she should tell him her dream. "The last full moon, I had a dream of a light. A light and a person-sized figure." She relayed her dream to him, but opted to leave out the part where she actually saw the floating light as she was awake. "I know there's something in there. As if the woods themselves are alive, pulling me closer." She popped another piece of pancake in her mouth and removed the one from the pan, pouring some more batter.

He looked away and rolled his eyes, careful to be sure she didn't see, though her back was still turned. He paused and finished up his last bite before speaking again. "Listen, I'm all for you following this...whatever it is, but this is turning into an obsession. Now you're dreaming about it?"

"It was one time!" she argued, slightly turning towards him, pancakes temporarily forgotten.

He held up his hands. "Do what you want, but I don't know what you're expecting to find out there. What if you step on a snake? What if you touch poison ivy? What if you trip and break your leg somewhere out there and I can't find you? Do you even know what's in those woods?"

Alyssa felt frustration rising inside her, but forced herself to calm down. "Drew," she said firmly, placing her hands on her hips as she turned to fully face him – a determined expression on her face. "I don't know what I'll find. Maybe I'll find nothing, maybe I'll find some lost treasure and we'll be rich." He rolled his eyes at that last bit. "All I know is that I can't ignore this. Support me or don't, but I'm going to do this regardless." With that, she turned back to the stove and continued cooking in silence.

They didn't speak much and mostly avoided each other until late afternoon, but their earlier argument weighed heavily on Alyssa's mind. She finally swallowed her pride and found Drew in his normal spot on the sofa. "I'm sorry," she said, looking at him.

He turned his attention from the TV to her and gave her a crooked grin, "Me too."

She reached down and kissed him on the cheek as she went about prepping for dinner. She had taken out some ground beef earlier to thaw, having planned to make a cottage pie for dinner. She set a large pot of water on the stove to boil. Grabbing some potatoes from the bin, she got to work peeling and cubing them. She plopped them into the now boiling water then grabbed a skillet to brown the meat. As she was cooking the meat, she felt arms wrap around her. She smiled and tilted her head up, looking at her husband. He took the opportunity and kissed her exposed neck. Chills ran down Alyssa's spine as her body slightly shuddered. "Babe! I'm busy," she giggled. He playfully smacked her on the backside and left the kitchen.

She finished with the meat and drained and mashed the potatoes. Assembling everything with a ton of cheese in a casserole dish, she placed it in the oven to bake. While she waited, she walked over to the living room and sat next to Drew. He was watching another sports show. Bored out of her mind, she grabbed her phone and began to aimlessly play a game.

Several minutes later, the timer beeped, signaling the dish was ready. She got up and took it out of the oven, setting it on a cooling rack. "Dinner's ready!" she called after a few minutes.

Drew met her in the kitchen expectantly. "Smells great," he said, inhaling deeply.

She scooped some up on a plate and handed it to him. He took it and sat at the bar as she served her own plate and followed. They ate in relative silence, enjoying the meal. Once they finished, Alyssa cleared the mess and put everything in the dishwasher. The pie was still too hot to put up, so she left it on the counter to finish cooling. Peeking outside to see if it was dark enough yet, her eyes sparkled. It was time.

CHAPTER 3

S tanding alone at the too familiar edge of the woods, Alyssa clutched her flashlight. Glancing up once more at the full moon, she took a deep breath. She grabbed a small tree and took an even smaller step forward. Shaking her head to clear her thoughts, she clicked on the flashlight and held her breath.

She took a step forward and entered the woods.

She paused. Nothing changed; all was silent. No Boogeyman suddenly came out to get her. No shining orb greeted her. What was she so afraid of before? The house was within eyesight, so if anything were to happen, her biggest challenge would be to run out without tripping over tree roots or getting tangled in vines.

Stepping forward, she continued to feel the familiar pull, almost as if there was a rope attached to her chest. Carefully avoiding roots, briars, and other unknown plants, she ventured deeper.

The lights of dozens of fireflies slowly blinked, giving a mysterious aura to the already enigmatic woods. A gentle breeze rustled the leaves, adding a slight chill to the air.

Slowly making her way deeper into the woods, she stopped to be sure the house was still in view. The last thing she needed was to get lost in here. She leaned against a tree, trying to figure out which direction to go. Left, right, straight ahead? The pull wasn't helpful as to which way to turn, so she continued straight ahead. "Maybe I should have left a trail of breadcrumbs," she whispered to herself, her own voice spooking her.

The pulling in her chest continued relentlessly. Shining her flashlight around, she saw nothing of interest; no reason to feel the way she was feeling. Looking back again, the house was now almost out of sight. She gave up and turned around, heading home for the night, pondering how to keep herself from getting lost next time.

She walked into the house to find Drew finishing up in the kitchen. "Oh!" she exclaimed. "You picked up! Thank you."

"Not like I don't live here, too."

"I'll remember that when the floors need mopping and the laundry needs folding," she teased.

"Maybe it's time I move out," he teased back.

"Be my guest. Then who's going to split the chores with you?"

"Hmm." He walked over to her and wrapped his arms around her waist with a smirk. "Maybe I'll have to keep you then."

She rolled her eyes at him. "How gracious of you. Thank you so much."

He gave her a peck on the forehead and walked towards the living room. "So, how did tonight go?"

"I made it inside. Felt the pull, but didn't want to get lost, so just went until I could barely see the house and turned around." She sat next to him on the sofa. "I need to figure out a way to not get lost in there."

"So you found...?"

"Nothing. Absolutely nothing," she said flatly.

"Well, that's disappointing I'm sure. What's the plan now?"

"I've got to learn the woods. I'll probably start exploring them more during the day or maybe clearing a path so even if I do get lost, I'll be able to find my way back."

"Clearing a path? And how do you suggest we go about doing that?" He looked at her with skepticism in his eyes.

"Well clearly with a machete," she laughed.

"Right, let's trust you with a machete. Gotcha. Great plan. How about we use the weed-wacker instead? Maybe a small chainsaw for the thinner trees?"

"I don't want to cut much down. Just enough to navigate through. Maybe 2 feet wide? That way we don't have to cut any trees or really do much." Just the thought of cutting into the woods hurt her heart. "Wait, did I hear you right? *We*?"

Drew rolled his eyes. "Like you can handle this by yourself," he grumbled. "Not that I want to get involved."

She threw her arms around him and continued. "What about putting hay down?"

"That's a lot of hay. Seriously, it is. How long are you wanting to make this path? What about poisoning the underbrush so it's dirt?"

"No!" Fear suddenly shot through her. "We can't poison anything! Do you realize how bad that is for the ground, the water, the animals, everything?" The woods were alive and she couldn't do more damage to them than they were already planning.

He put up his hands. "Okay, okay, no poison, got it. So, we'll just weed-wack and put down hay for now."

"I can live with that. Let's start Saturday! That way we have time to grab enough hay to line the path over the next couple of days."

He groaned. "How do I get myself into these situations?"

"You've been saying you need to go outside more, so this is your chance!" She nudged his arm with a wink.

"Sure, let's just ignore the deadly spiders and venomous snakes."

"That's the spirit! Don't mess with them and they won't mess with you." She smiled brightly.

Drew, exasperated, sighed and ran a hand through his hair. "Fine. But you're helping with the hay. I'm not carrying it all."

"Deal!" she said excitedly, grinning from ear to ear. It wasn't often they worked on projects together, so this would be a great bonding experience for them as well. Flipping through the channels, he put on a game show and they playfully competed against each other.

An hour or so later, forgetting her disappointment from not getting very far in the woods earlier, Alyssa's excitement kept her awake. She had grand visions of a small trail snaking through the woods, heading deeper and deeper. Biting her lip to keep from grinning again, she forced her mind to shut down and finally fall asleep.

The following Saturday, after a quick breakfast, they headed to the shed outside. Drew grabbed the weed-wacker and replaced the plastic strings with metal blades. Alyssa found a large pair of garden sheers and a well-used set of loppers. The sun shone brightly in the sky, illuminating the underbrush beautifully.

"Alright boss," Drew said as he started up the trimmer. "Where do you want this path?"

Alyssa briefly pondered, eyes landing on the perfect spot. "There!" She pointed to a spot about three feet wide with large trees on either side at the very edge of the woods that she used last time she walked into the forest. Drew walked over and revved up the trimmer, clearing the sparse grass and briars.

As he cleared off the small plants, Alyssa went behind him and cut the thin saplings that the trimmer couldn't cut down, even with the metal blades. It was a beautiful day; hardly a cloud in the sky with a gentle breeze rustling the leaves on the treetops above their heads.

Every so often they would take a break and walk back to sit on the front porch, just enjoying the day. "So, how much farther do you want to go?" he asked, taking a swig of water from a bottle.

"How much hay do we have?"

"Good question. We should probably start putting it down to see how far we can reach." He finished his water and stood up. "Ready?"

"I was born ready!"

He rolled his eyes at her with a smile.

They began the daunting task of unloading, carrying, and spreading the hay. After a few more small breaks, they managed to fill the entire path they had trimmed with hay and still had some to spare.

"Can we keep going until we run out?" Alyssa batted her eyelashes at Drew.

"You owe me," he grumbled as he started the weed-wacker again. After a few minutes, he stopped and called her over. "Look at these flowers. Do you want to keep them?"

"Oh, they're beautiful! Though I have no idea what they are. Let's leave them for the bees. Can we trim around them?"

"Sure. Just checking. Don't need you mad at me if you saw them just lying there after I cut them."

They resumed their work and as the path was getting longer and longer, Alyssa felt her excitement build. Another hour passed and they decided to quit for the day after running out of hay.

After showers and dinner, they collapsed on the sofa. "We did good today," she said, beaming at Drew and giving him a kiss on the cheek. "Thank you so much."

"Remember how I said you owed me?" He raised an eyebrow. "I'd like to cash that in."

"Oh geez, what do you want?" her mind immediately thinking of the bedroom.

"Well, what I'd really like is for us to go into the bedroom, you to take off my shirt while I take off yours," he paused, giving her a look. She raised an eyebrow in response, waiting for him to continue. "Maybe take off some more clothes...and you to..." he paused again, clearly enjoying himself. "...to give me the best massage of my life. Because, man, am I sore."

She nudged him with her elbow. "Why do I have to be topless for that, pervert?"

"Just a perk," he grinned at her with faux innocence. "Okay and maybe have some wild and crazy sex after," he said with a wink.

"Oh no, who could have seen that coming? Fine," she said with exaggerated exasperation. "Let's go."

Drew seemed to suddenly have more energy than he did all day as he jumped up and quickly walked to the bedroom. Alyssa smiled and sighed as she turned off the TV. "Be there in a minute!" she called. "I need to shut down in here." After she was through, she walked to the bedroom and slowly slid off her nightshirt, letting it fall to the floor.

Drew stared at her, hunger in his eyes as she sauntered over. He lay on the bed, already naked, erect penis ready, waiting, forgetting his earlier request of a massage. She crawled onto the bed and leaned over him, purposefully breathing her hot breath over him, causing him to shudder.

"Come here," he demanded. She obeyed and he quickly removed her panties and pushed two fingers inside her. She cried out, though she wasn't sure if it was surprise, pleasure, pain, or all three. He began thrusting in and out of her, feeling her begin to get wet for him. She bit her lip and shut her eyes, tilting her head towards the ceiling.

He suddenly stopped and roughly moved her to sit on top of him. She ground her hips in a circle and stifled a moan as he watched, loving the expression on her face. He suddenly grabbed her hips and began thrusting in and out of her. She yelped in surprise, but quickly recovered. As quickly as he started, he stopped. "Bend over," he said gruffly. She got from on top of him and bent down on all fours. He grabbed her hips and slammed into her. Biting her bottom lip hard, she enjoyed the slight pain. He wasn't usually gentle, but not this rough; tonight he seemed different.

He pounded into her and grabbed a fistful of her long hair. She let out a cry as he pulled back. She tried squirming out from his grasp, but he held tighter. With each thrust he yanked on her hair. Her scalp was on fire. "Drew," she panted, "Stop." He released her hair, but didn't immediately stop thrusting.

He pulled out and turned her over, forcing her back into missionary. His hands found her neck and he held on. Anticipating this, Alyssa didn't struggle but instead ran her fingernails down his back. This caused his grip to tighten. Slight panic welled up inside her, but she forced it down, knowing he wouldn't hurt her. His grip continued to tighten as he thrust into her harder and faster. He looked down at his wife, her face turning red. He released her and pulled out.

"Take it," he commanded as he lay on his back. She silently opened her mouth and put the length of him in her mouth. She twirled her tongue around him as she moved up and down, causing a low moan to escape his lips. He suddenly grabbed her head and forced her down as he thrust into her mouth. Startled, she pulled back, but he held her tight. She couldn't move as he thrust in and out so hard he caused her to gag. He continued holding her as she made noises in her throat, trying to get him to release her. She pressed her arms against him and pushed up, but he just wound his fingers in her hair, holding onto her tighter. He thrust one more time and held her head down so hard she couldn't breathe. He moaned loudly as she struggled. She felt his hot cum fill her throat and mouth and began gagging, but he held firm. He finally released her and she began coughing, trying to catch her breath.

"Drew, what the actual fuck is wrong with you?" she shouted, still coughing.

He lay there panting, body sweaty, and gave her a grin. "Told you I wanted wild sex tonight."

"That wasn't wild, Drew, that was cruel. Don't ever fucking do that again or I swear I'll bite your dick off."

"Oh, come on baby," he said, turning towards her. "You know you liked it."

Alyssa didn't say a word. While not her first love interest, Drew had been her first sexual partner and she wasn't sure if she was just being a prude or a bad wife by not liking what had just happened. She stayed silent as she lay down, not facing him. He closed the distance between them and wrapped his arms around her.

He had been rough in the past and she enjoyed it, but tonight seemed different. For one, he had never trapped her before while she was sucking him. Two, though he had his hands on her neck other times, he had never squeezed quite so hard. She frowned and closed her eyes, hoping to move on from the night.

Her brain didn't allow her to fall asleep, her mind racing from what had just happened. She thought back to recent times they had sex. Those were tender, sweet, and more along the lines of lovemaking than anything. Not...whatever just happened. She bit her lip, unsure of how to feel.

Her thoughts traveled to the beginnings of their relationship five years ago. They met on a dating app – two kindred spirits not too far apart from one another. Who knew there would be love to be found in this little town? He had been so gentle with her, so affectionate, so caring. He owned the house, while she was living in an apartment, so it only made sense for her to move in with him when things got serious.

She thought back to when he took her virginity. Even then she didn't feel as she did tonight. Tonight she felt fear, panic, and now confusion. Maybe it was a one-off situation. Maybe he just needed to let out some steam. She hoped this was one-and-done and not the beginning of something.

Forcing her thoughts away, she turned her focus to the woods. Though she had been feeling the call for months, it took her longer than she expected to discuss it with her husband. Thinking back on it, she felt silly keeping it from him, but still not knowing what it is isn't helping anything. Strange pulling feeling in her chest? Check. Only happens during the full moon? Check. Walking through the creepy woods at night? Not so much.

She mulled over the idea that it could be supernatural. Some unseen force calling her into the dark to devour her soul. She rolled her eyes at her own thoughts. Demons and devils had bigger fish to fry than her.

"What do you think it is?" she remembered Drew asking.

"I have no idea," she replied sheepishly. *"But I'm going to find out."*

A smile graced her lips as she remembered her determination that night. Sleep finally taking her, she dreamed of fireflies, soft wind, and a full moon.

CHAPTER 4

T he next day, Alyssa pushed away what happened the previous night and managed to convince Drew to go back into the woods to continue with the path. "...and I want solar lights lining it and...Drew are you even listening to me?"

Drew nodded, carrying the tools down the trail. "Yep, I hear you. Solar lights. Do you realize how expensive those things are? I'd imagine you're looking to light the entire path. You know, the whole *several hundred feet* of it?"

"Of course! Why not? Go big or go home!"

"Maybe," he grumbled as they reached where they stopped yesterday. They began clearing again, watching the brush transform from unmanageable to, well, slightly more manageable.

After a long, exhausting day of deciding where and how exactly Alyssa wanted the remainder of path and then the daunting task of clearing a spot large enough for her to place a bench, she and Drew plopped onto the sofa.

"I don't see what you see in those trees. They're just trees. We traveled all throughout the woods and there was nothing. Absolutely nothing but trees, trees, and more trees. Oh and thorns, lots of thorns." He held up his arm, full of scratches.

She gently grabbed his arm and kissed it. "There, all better." He rolled his eyes at her. "I don't know what it is I feel. I can't explain it.

Imagine a rope, I guess. A rope tied around your torso and someone is gently pulling on it."

"I know. You keep saying that. But it doesn't make any sense. Why only at night? Why only during the full moon? What are you, a werewolf?"

"Maybe I am! It's my ancestral call. Maybe there's a pack in the woods. Better watch out, I'll eat you!" She laughed at him.

"Yeah, yeah. All fun and games until your fangs sink into my flesh," he grumbled, staring at the TV.

"Well, then you'll just turn and we can be together forever. Bwahahaha." She put up her hands to look like claws and bared her teeth.

He glanced at her out the side of his eye. "Now who's being ridiculous?" he scoffed.

"What's ridiculous about it? It was your idea," she pouted.

"Forever's a long time. I thought it was till death do us part?"

"Wow. Ouch. Okay." The twinge of pain in her heart felt like a minor shockwave as she fell silent. He didn't say a word.

Things were going so well. She didn't understand what happened. She knew he was sore and hurting from the two days of being hunched over the weed-wacker, swaying it back and forth for hours at a time, but that didn't excuse his comment. She decided to wait it out a few more minutes and see if he said anything or realized she was hurt before heading to bed. As she suspected, he was silent.

"I'm exhausted," she said, standing up. "I'm going to bed. Are you coming?"

"No, I'm not tired yet," he replied, still looking at the TV.

Alyssa tried to hide the small frown that appeared on her face. "Okay, well just please be quiet when you come in. I'll probably be asleep." She walked over and gave him a kiss goodnight, highly disappointed in the turn of events.

She lay in bed, their conversation replaying in her head. Or rather their lack of conversation. He hadn't ever said anything like that before. Was he unhappy? Did she do something wrong? She thought they were having a good time. Then there was the sex the other night. Something was off.

He hadn't come to bed yet, though it was a work night. She would have thought he would be exhausted, ready for bed immediately after showering. She glanced at the clock – midnight. Deciding to go check on him, she went out into the living room where she found him asleep on the sofa. Her heart sank further. *What did I do?*

She debated waking him up, weighing the pros and cons, but decided against it and went back to bed. She tossed and turned until the exhaustion from the day's activities caught up to her and she fell into a hard sleep.

Chapter 5

She awoke to her alarm chiming at 7 a.m., its gentle melody softly pulling her from her slumber. She felt that she was alone in the bed and sighed. Getting up, she immediately went to check on Drew, who was still sleeping. She walked over and nudged him. "Hey," she said softly. "It's time to get up. You have work today."

His eyes opened a crack as he groaned. "Five more minutes."

"No, I'm sorry, but you need to get up. We need money and for that to happen, we both need to get to work."

"Ugh. Fine." He wasn't usually this much of a grouch in the morning. He stood up and stretched, making grunting noises as his joints popped – likely stiff from sleeping on the sofa.

"I'm throwing a sausage biscuit in the microwave. Do you want one?" Alyssa tried to act like everything was normal.

"I'm good," he said curtly.

She turned away and hid the dejected look on her face as he walked towards the bathroom. Popping some coffee grounds into the single-serve coffee maker, she began her morning ritual. Coffee and breakfast, watering the plants on the porch, putting the dirty dishes from breakfast in the dishwasher, washing her face, brushing her teeth, then finally getting ready for work. In that order every day. Drew always finished before her. He seemed in a daze when he left. He gave her a kiss and walked out, nearly forgetting to verbalize goodbye.

She tightly shut her eyes after he left. "I won't let this ruin my day," she promised herself. She forced herself to smile and take on the day.

Alyssa's commute to work was uneventful and she arrived without incident, though her mind wasn't on the road. Saying good morning to her coworkers as she walked past, she made it to her desk and gingerly sat down. Glancing at the photo of her and Drew smiling and having a good time made her heart ache.

She shook her head. *Stop being ridiculous. This is one small misunderstanding. He was probably just tired and fell asleep.* As for the comment, he likely didn't even remember saying it. At least that's what she was trying to convince herself.

She was incredibly grateful for her job working in the small town's only insurance agency. Before she moved from Timmal, the nearby big city, she had been a customer service representative for one of the larger agencies in the area. Luckily, that experience helped her nab this position so she didn't have to commute as far every day. Hours passed as she carried on with her normal work: Monday meetings, spreadsheets, listening to coworkers gossip about their weekend, assisting clients with their insurance claims and frantic calls. Her favorite coworker and close friend, the Marketing Manager, Jasmine, walked up to her in the break room during lunch. "Okay, what's wrong with you?" She stood with her arms folded as she stared at Alyssa.

"Nothing! Well, Drew is acting weird, but seriously, it's minor and isn't an issue." She smiled at Jasmine.

"Weird how? As weird as you've been acting all day?"

"What do you mean? I haven't done anything."

"Alyssa, I know you better than you know yourself. That or you're lying to me. I can't tell which one right now. You've been quiet; abnormally quiet."

"You know, some of us actually have real work to do," Alyssa made a playfully mocking face at her friend.

"Whatever." Jasmine waved her hand in the air and dismissed her comment. "Tell me about Drew. What happened?"

Jasmine didn't know about the strange calling Alyssa felt. She had to come up with something to avoid that topic, but still give Jasmine what she's looking for. Not even catching that Jasmine already knew who caused the problem before Alyssa said it, she softly started, "Long story short, he made a comment." She paused. "Said something along the lines of marriage being till death do us part when I mentioned us being together forever if we turned into werewolves."

Jasmine gave Alyssa a look. "Werewolves, really? I swear you two have the strangest conversations. Either way that's an odd thing to say. Has he been acting distant? Making any other comments? Acting funny?"

"Well, he slept on the sofa last night."

"Did you kick him out of the bed?"

"No, he just didn't come to bed. I don't know what's going on. Maybe I'm overthinking this." Alyssa sighed.

"We all know how he's going to react if you ask him about it. I'd just ignore it for now, but watch him carefully. See if he makes any other comments or starts acting strangely."

"Doesn't that seem a little, I don't know, Jazz, unhealthy?" She gave her friend a pointed look.

"You call it unhealthy; I call it avoiding confrontation."

"I don't like confrontation either, but I can't just ignore this. I'm going to talk to him tonight." She finished her lunch and stood up to go back to her desk.

"Okay," Jasmine said. "Just don't haunt me if you get murdered."

Alyssa rolled her eyes and walked away, equally grateful and irritated at Jasmine's response.

Back at her desk, Alyssa checked the clock and sighed when she realized she still had half an hour of lunch left. She *could* start working again, but her mind started to wander. She thought of her parents and their strained relationship – she couldn't call them for advice. Not when they haven't spoken in over six months.

Her thoughts then drifted to her own future children and she vowed to never let history repeat itself. She smiled when picturing a little boy and a little girl running around their property, laughing as they came back, presenting mud pies to her and Drew.

Drew. All thoughts of children disappeared as the evening weekend events came crashing down on her, sending ice through her veins. She had always been strong-willed, but felt so helpless when he took over. She realized how helpless she really was in that situation; how much control he had over her. She tightly shut her eyes, ignoring the uncomfortable feeling of anxiety creeping up on her. Not one for being controlled, she planned to confront him about his actions.

Opening her eyes, she checked the clock again. Five more minutes. She decided it was time to put her personal thoughts aside and start working. Just as she placed her fingers to the keyboard, the phone rang. She put on her best customer service voice and answered, slipping seamlessly back into her role.

CHAPTER 6

Alyssa arrived home before Drew, as usual. Her commute was much shorter than his, so it was to be expected. Though her nerves were getting the better of her, she started on dinner. He usually cooked on weekdays, but she was hoping this would brighten his mood. He walked through the door as her back was turned.

"You're cooking again?" he asked incredulously. "Is it my birthday?"

She scoffed. "I'm capable you know." He came up behind her, wrapped his arms around her waist, and gave her a kiss on the cheek. He let go and walked towards the fridge to grab a beer.

So far so good. Much better than this morning. Maybe she should let it go. He probably had too much on his mind and his body was likely exhausted from helping her clear the path.

No. She couldn't just let this sit.

"Hey Drew?"

"Hmm?"

"About last night...what happened?"

He turned towards her, eyeing her apprehensively. "What do you mean?"

"Well for one, you slept on the sofa. For two, you made that comment about marriage only lasting until death. I realize nothing is forever, but that hurt." She was still facing the stove, so he was unable to see her face.

"I wasn't tired when you went to bed, but must have been more tired than I thought. That wasn't intentional. Neither was hurting you. I don't really remember exactly what I said, but I'm sorry. I didn't mean for you to be so upset. I really just remember talking about werewolves." He put down his beer and walked towards her. He gently turned her around. "Baby, I mean it. I'm really sorry." He gave her a hug and a kiss on the forehead. "You know I don't always think before I speak."

"It felt different this time. It's like you weren't really there. I just want to understand."

Drew stepped back and ran his hand through his hair. "I honestly didn't mean anything by it. I truly don't even remember what I said and I'm sorry. I was probably just zoned out and more tired than I thought."

"Are you sure you aren't having doubts? Doubts about us?" Alyssa bit her lip.

"It's not like that!" he exclaimed, beginning to get frustrated. "I love you, Alyssa. I truly do. Please believe me when I say that whatever it was, it was just a passing comment."

"Okay," she said softly. He gave her a kiss and another hug, which she returned, but still felt a little hurt. Maybe she just needed to sleep it off. He did apologize after all. She served dinner and they ate, talking about their day, though she left out the part about Jasmine and her advice to keep quiet. He didn't seem to be her biggest fan.

The rest of their week was uneventful – work seemed normal for both, they discussed where they wanted to go on vacation, Alyssa picked up painting and began honing her skills. She forgave Drew, chalking it up to him just being tired, but as the days went by, she couldn't shake the feeling that something was on Drew's mind. She tried brushing it off, but her heart knew something was wrong.

One evening when they were both sitting on the sofa together, Alyssa couldn't take it anymore and finally addressed it. "Drew?"

He peeled his eyes away from the TV and looked at her, giving her his full attention.

"Are you really okay? You've been off, but I can't place what it is." She carefully watched his expression, searching for answers.

His face darkened, but he quickly regained composure. "I don't know. I guess I'm just stressed at work. You know, deadlines, expectations. Maybe it's affecting me more than I let on."

"Let's talk about it then!" she said brightly. "You know you're not alone."

"I'd rather not burden you with my boring problems," he smiled, but it didn't quite reach his eyes.

"Baby, you're not burdening me. We're a team, remember? Your problems are my problems and I want to be there for you."

"A team." He lightly chuckled and leaned back, running his hands through his hair again. "I just need to figure some things out."

"Like what?" she asked, getting slightly nervous.

"Well, I guess what I want in life," he said softly, staring off into the distance. Her heart skipped a beat as her breath caught in her throat. "I want so much more than what I've become. I want to travel. I want to experience more of life, but I just feel stuck."

A tear rolled down her cheeks. "Drew...I..."

"Oh my God, I see how that came out. No! No, baby, please don't think I feel stuck with you! I love you. I need you. I'm such an idiot. I hate that I say stupid things. I hate that I hurt you unintentionally." His face displayed a slight panicked expression.

Alyssa felt a mixture of relief and worry as she wiped the tears from her face. "Let's figure this out together," she offered.

His expression relaxed, still looking away. "I'd like that," he said softly, finally facing her. He reached up and gently touched her cheek. "I'm so sorry."

She gave him a small smile. "No, it was my fault for jumping to conclusions and making it about me."

"What if I promise to try to communicate better? No locking things up inside, no more secrets, just honesty."

Secrets? she thought to herself then said aloud, "What secrets?"

"Nothing," he said quickly. "I just meant it as a figure of speech."

Alyssa felt there was more than what he was saying. "What happened to honesty?" She unconsciously pulled herself into the corner of the sofa and away from him. "What are you not saying?"

"Please don't shy away from me. I'm trying, I really am."

"Then just spit it out!" she cried, tears beginning to roll down her face again.

Drew's eyes widened as he put his hands up. "Alyssa, I..."

"Just tell me the truth!" Her heart was racing and the tears were flowing down her face again.

His shoulders slumped, defeated. "Okay." He reached over and grabbed her hand. "I've been thinking. Doing a lot of thinking actually." He paused. "I don't want you to think less of me for this." She kept quiet, expecting the worst. "I've been thinking about my career. I've been in the same routine for so long that I just can't stand it. I don't know if I want to stay where I'm at. I don't know where I would go or what I'd want to do..." He trailed off.

She was momentarily silent. "That's it? You're worried I'm going to judge you because you're unhappy at work?"

"It's more than just being unhappy at work. It's fear for our future. What I have now is stable, it's comfortable-"

"It's just not fulfilling or making you happy," she said quietly. Her tears stopping.

"Right. What if I make the wrong decision? What if the grass isn't greener on the other side? I can't risk your future just because I'm, what, going through a crisis or something? I don't want to drag you along or screw up your plans because I'm lost right now."

"Baby. You need to remember that we. Are. A. Team," she accentuated each word carefully. "I want your happiness just as much as you want mine." She squeezed his hand. "Plans can change. We grow; we adapt. But let's do it together, okay?"

He smiled softly and nodded. "Okay," he agreed.

She turned towards the TV and moved to lean her head on his shoulder as he laid his head on top of hers. They both smiled, feeling the weight lift from their shoulders.

After a restful night's sleep, morning arrived and Alyssa was feeling oddly chipper. She and Drew got ready for the day, parted ways, and went on their merry way to work. Knowing Alyssa's roundabout schedule, Jasmine was waiting for her, leaning against the doorway to the building.

"Good morning, sunshine!" Alyssa called.

Jasmine narrowed her eyes at her. "What's wrong with you?"

"Nothing; just happy it's finally Friday."

Shrugging, Jasmine moved to stand beside her friend. "Okay, so," she began. "I'm thinking we need to do something together! It's been so long since I've heard of you going out and you could use a good girl's night."

"I'm listening," Alyssa said, raising her eyebrow and slightly smiling.

"What if we went to one of those boozy painting classes?"

"The ones where you drink and paint a picture?"

"Yes! Exactly!"

"Where's the closest studio? I doubt we have anything like that here."

"Not here, but in Timmal."

"Hmm, okay! I'm in! Who's going? What time?"

"Slow down there, girl! I haven't gotten that far, yet," Jasmine said, laughing.

"Okay, okay, but you'd better figure it out soon. Don't you have to make reservations for that?"

"Crap, that's right. I forgot about that. What about just us two? I'll look and see what times they have. Do you have anything in particular you want to paint?"

"Girl, I don't even know what they offer. You pick everything and just let me know what time and where and I'll be there."

"You got it! I'm so excited! We haven't gone out together in ages!"

Alyssa laughed with a grin on her face, her friend's enthusiasm infectious. "It's time for us to get to work now! Don't want to be late."

"Hopefully the day passes by quickly," Jasmine said earnestly.

As luck would have it, the day seemed to drag on for both of them. At their lunch break, Jasmine made the reservations while Alyssa texted Drew, letting him know her plans. As they ate, Alyssa looked at what they'd be painting that night – a beautiful sunset over dark trees of a forest. She smiled, thinking how appropriate the painting was given her pull towards the woods.

Alyssa rushed home after work, eager to change into more comfortable clothes and prepare for the night. She packed a bottle of wine and some small snacks. As she finished, Drew walked in from work.

"Hey babe," she called.

"Looks like you're planning on a fun night." He offered a smile, but it didn't quite reach his eyes.

She didn't notice, but continued flitting around the kitchen, preparing for a quick meal.

"Yep! I'm super excited for this. I haven't gone out in so long and with getting into painting now, this is the perfect girls night!"

He lightly chuckled and walked to the bedroom to change.

Alyssa left an hour later, having impatiently waited on time to tick by faster.

The night went off without a hitch and when Alyssa arrived home, Drew was already asleep in bed. She showered and joined him, still on a high from her night with Jasmine.

Chapter 7

The next day, Alyssa and Drew finished lining the path with hay. Once that was done, they carried a bench into the woods to place in the cleared circle and positioned solar lights around it.

"Isn't this cozy?!" Alyssa exclaimed.

"When exactly do you plan on using this bench?" Drew asked skeptically.

"When I come in here at night, of course," she said in a matter-of-fact tone.

"Right," he said sarcastically. "Because walking down a dark path in the woods in the middle of the night, barely lit up by solar lights, just to come sit on a bench sounds like a great time. Sign me up."

"It isn't for you," she said, giving him a pointed look. "You know the full moon is coming up and this will be the perfect place to be when I finally figure out what's been calling me!"

"Yeah. You and the bears and the raccoons and the spiders and the-"

"I get it, Drew," she sighed.

"Just don't come haunt me when you get killed. I'm petty enough to say I told you so."

"Sadly, I know you are. But nothing is going to happen!" Exasperated, she finished placing the solar lights around the circle. "Perfect!"

"Did you even test those to be sure they'll get enough light in here?" Drew asked, raising an eyebrow at her.

"...yes," she lied. "I definitely did do that. Yep, exactly that."

He rolled his eyes at her. "Of course you didn't. Oh well, at least we didn't buy enough to line the entire trail just yet. These will be a good tester." He grabbed her hand and spun her around the clearing.

"What's this all about?" she laughed.

"Just happy to see you so excited about this," he beamed at her.

"I couldn't have done it without you," she smiled up at him, planting a kiss on his lips.

"Ready to go back to the house?"

"Yep. I think we're finished here. Nothing left to do except learn these woods before the calling hits again."

"Let's head back then," he said as he grabbed her hand, gently leading her towards the house.

Later that night, she glanced out a few windows, trying to get an angle to see whether the lights had charged, but the clearing was too deep in the woods. She gave up and made a mental note to move some of the lights closer to the tree line tomorrow so she could see how bright they shine. "Or I guess I could always go into the woods tonight to see them in person," she murmured.

"What?" Drew asked from the living room.

"I can't see the solar lights from here. Do you want to come with me down the trail to see how they work?"

"Can we bring a flashlight at least?" Drew asked, flipping his head around to look at her.

"Of course! It's cloudy out and way too dark without that."

"Sure, I'll come."

Together, they walked out, hand in hand, each holding a flashlight with their free hand. They made it to the edge of the path, but Alyssa stopped.

"What's wrong?" Drew asked.

"I'm scared," she admitted.

"Incredible. The woman who is planning on coming into the woods – *alone* – in the middle of the night to sit – *alone* – on a bench – did I mention *alone* – is scared?"

"Not of the darkness or the woods," she scoffed. "Okay, maybe a little." Drew chuckled. "What if this isn't everything I thought it would be? What if this whole several weekslong project we worked on together was for nothing?"

"You aren't just talking about going to see the lights anymore, are you? How about you don't worry about that for now and focus on finding your way to the clearing at night. Then you can worry about the other stuff."

Alyssa nodded, unsure if he could even see her head move in the dark, and took a step forward. He stepped aside for her to go first. "Lead the way, captain." He held his arm out in front of them, leading down the dark trail.

She took a breath and began walking, looking slightly down at the winding path to be sure she didn't stray from the hay. They made it to the clearing to see most of the lights lit up. Alyssa sat on the bench, admiring how the light reflected on the tree bark and the leaves above.

"Looks like they work to me. Well, sorta," Drew said, sitting next to her.

"Mhm," she said under her breath, looking farther out beyond their little circle.

All was as calm as could be. The cicadas singing their songs, a faint breeze rustling the leaves on the trees, and the quiet beating of their two hearts.

"What are you looking for?" he asked, curiously.

"Well, remember how I saw that light? I'm wondering if I'll see it again. While it isn't constantly on my mind, I can't get it out of my head."

"And you're sure it wasn't just a firefly?" he asked dubiously.

"No, it was bigger than that."

"That's what you keep saying, but have you seen it since? I mean, we've been all throughout these woods over the past few weeks and we haven't seen any indication that someone was back here."

"I didn't expect there to be. If someone was here, they were just passing through. But I have a feeling it wasn't a person either. I'm sticking with my will-o'-the-wisp theory." She nodded once to prove her point, her jeweled pendant briefly shimmering in the glow of the lights.

"Okay Miss Wisp. Whatever you say. Can we go back inside now? I'm not as much of a fan of this as you are."

"Scared?" she teased.

"I'd call it more uncomfortable. I still don't know how you're going to do this alone."

"Just watch. You'll see."

"Hmm, you're right. We will see." With that, he grabbed her hand and stood up, walking down the trail out of the clearing.

Neither noticed a faint, almost mist-like figure standing just out of reach of the light.

As Alyssa and Drew made their way back down the path, the clearing slowly faded into the darkness behind them. The air was cool, yet pleasant. A strange silence seemed to follow them down the trail as their presence silenced the insects, the only sound was the crunching of fresh hay under their feet.

"You really believe that will-o'-the-wisp thing?" he asked.

"What other explanation is there? It wasn't a firefly. I'm 99% certain it wasn't a person. There's something about this place and a wisp would fit perfectly in here."

"Something about this place, huh?" he said. He then murmured, "That's what I'm afraid of."

They made it to the house and decided to retire for the night. After shutting down, Alyssa lay in bed, mind still spinning from the magic of the clearing. The flickering of the lights, the lull of the cicada song, the way her heart swelled when Drew agreed to go into the woods with her. She forced her mind to clear and finally fell asleep.

The next few days were a blur. The mornings and afternoons were the same as always: get up, breakfast, go to work, gossip with Jasmine, go home. Once Friday evening hit, the real fun began. The full moon was only a few days away and she needed to prepare.

Drew helped her line the trail with more solar lights and she spent what little sunlight was left to learn the path with each snaking twist and turn. Her mind was fixated on this upcoming full moon, when she hoped to finally understand what had been calling her.

"Not much longer now," she murmured to herself. She looked around for Drew, but didn't see him anywhere. Calling out to him, she wandered throughout the trail. When her search came up empty, she decided to go to the house in case she didn't hear him say that's where he was going. Walking in, she called his name, but didn't get a response.

Looking outside, she saw both vehicles were still in the driveway. Confused and slightly concerned, she walked back outside to find him sitting on the front porch. "Where were you?" she asked curiously, not seeing him as she walked past to go inside.

"In the shed," he replied smoothly, putting his hands behind his head.

Alyssa slightly scrunched up her face. "How long have you been sitting here? You didn't hear me calling you?"

He looked up at her, furrowing his eyebrows. "I just sat down and no, I don't think I heard anything. But then again, I was lost in my own thoughts."

"Thinking about what?" she asked, sitting down on the chair next to him, reaching out her hand to hold his.

He didn't reach back, but stared off in the distance. "I know the full moon is coming up and I'm slightly worried." He turned his head towards her and Alyssa gave him a look. "Okay, more than slightly. I really don't want you going into the woods alone. You're not afraid? I don't just mean of the darkness, but of what may be hiding in there?"

"Sure I am. Who isn't afraid of the unknown?" she pulled her hand back, pretending she didn't notice his lack of physical affection.

"What if you find secrets that'll change your life?"

There was that word again. Secrets.

Alyssa raised an eyebrow and gave him a skeptical look. "You know, for someone who didn't believe in this, you're sure starting to sound concerned."

"Is it a crime to worry about my wife?"

"No, but it seems deeper than that. What are you afraid of?"

He paused and shifted his eyes to the woods then back on her. "Just you getting hurt," he said quickly.

He's acting strange again, she thought to herself as she studied his face. "I thought you were okay with this? For months you haven't really said much about it, but now it seems like you're trying to talk me out of it."

His jaw was tight and his brow was furrowed. "I guess now that it's here, I'm starting to see how reckless it is," he said, a strange tone to his voice. "You're planning on sitting alone in a clearing in the woods at night. It would be bad enough during the day."

"It's not like it'll be completely dark. We have all the lights installed," she argued back.

"That's not the point. You don't know what might be watching you; what's out there. What if this whole thing isn't as innocent as it seems?"

Alyssa laughed softly, trying to lighten the mood. "What is this, a horror movie? I mean I get it, we live on several acres and have hardly any neighbors, there are lots of dark wooded areas, oh, and we can't forget about the spooky shed." She paused, cracking a smile. "Thinking about it, it really is the perfect setting for a horror movie."

Drew rolled his eyes at her. "This isn't a joke," the frustration evident in his voice.

She frowned, pulling her legs up on the chair. "I've been planning this too long to back out now. Please understand that I have to do this."

He ran his hand through his hair and sighed. "Stubborn as always." With that, he stood up and walked inside, roughly shutting the door behind him, leaving Alyssa slightly stunned on the porch.

CHAPTER 8

Alyssa sat on the porch a while longer, lost in her thoughts. She couldn't figure out how or why he has been so hot and cold. What's been causing his sudden mood shifts? He told her before that it was his career, but there's something more to this and she was determined to get to the bottom of it.

Staring unconsciously at the solar lights in the trail, she noticed them going dark and back on again – almost as if something was walking in front of them. Something big.

Her mind immediately went to a bear, but as far as she knew, there weren't any in this area. Looking around, she didn't see any lights that would indicate someone was on the property. *It was probably a raccoon*, she thought to herself, ignoring the fact that raccoons are nowhere near as large as this figure seemed to be.

She realized her fear would probably get the better of her in the next couple of days if she ignored it. Walking towards the woods, Alyssa bit her lip, pulled out her phone, and turned on the flashlight. She realized whatever was there would likely run away as she approached, but she had to at least try to figure out what she had seen.

After a few minutes of searching along the tree line and finding absolutely nothing, she gave up. She walked back to the house and went inside to find Drew in his normal spot on the sofa watching TV.

"Hey," she said. "Thanks for helping me again today."

"Mhm," he barely replied.

"You're distant again." She decided to come right out and say it. No use beating around the bush.

"Have you always been this much of a nag?" He turned his head to look at her out the side of his narrowed eyes.

Taken aback, Alyssa wasn't sure what to say. Not wanting to start a fight, she held back the comment on the tip of her tongue about him nagging her just minutes ago. "That was rude," was all she could get out.

He continued watching TV, not bothering to respond to her.

"Drew!" she said, growing more frustrated. She grabbed the remote and shut off the TV.

"What the fuck, Alyssa?" he yelled. "Didn't I do enough for you today? I can't have this one pleasure?"

Now extremely hurt, Alyssa tossed the remote back towards him and walked away. As she made her way towards the bedroom, her heart raced with a mixture of confusion and anger. It was as if he was looking for a fight.

She leaned against the doorframe, trying to process what had just happened. She thought back to their day today. He cooked breakfast, they watched some TV, then went outside for a few chores. After the chores were finished, they put the remaining solar lights along the trail and she went inside the woods. He apparently went into the shed while she did that, but she couldn't imagine what could have happened there that would have caused this big of a change in him.

She couldn't keep up with his constant mood swings. Trying to make a connection, she thought back to when they first started. It was probably around the time she started feeling the pulling in the woods. Could that be it? It did seem highly coincidental that whenever he acted strangely, she would see something that night.

She shook her head, dispelling the thought. There was no connection between woods and her husband, so why try tying his mood to shadows and potential bears? A tear slipped down her cheek; something that was becoming too common.

She was pulled from her thoughts by a soft knock. Looking up, she wiped her face. "What do you want?" she said dejectedly.

"Can we talk? Please?"

"There's nothing to say. You aren't interested in sharing what you have going on, so why should I try?"

"I'm sorry," he sighed. "I don't have an excuse for how I acted. I've been so overwhelmed with my own thoughts lately."

"Overwhelmed? How about coming to me instead of shutting me out?"

He stepped closer, his eyes pleading. "There are things in my life that I just can't talk about right now. Please understand. I'm not doing any of this to hurt you. I'm just scared."

Her frustration was barely masked now. "Scared of what? You can't expect me to sit around, waiting for you to deal with whatever this is on your own."

He ran a hand through his hair. "I'm trying. Believe me when I say I am. I just don't want to drag you into anything."

"It's a little late for that," she said bitterly. "You've dragged me in and shut me out at the same time." She got up and looked out the window, half expecting to see something again. The silent tension hung thick and heavy. "I know we can figure this out together, but you have to let me in," she said quietly.

"I want to," Drew said, unmoving. "Trust me, I really do, but I can't. Just...give me some time, okay?"

Time, she thought. She nodded, not looking at him. She wanted to fix this, but the distance growing between them was impossible to ignore. "Just don't take too long or I might not wait around." She closed her eyes, realizing she actually meant what she said.

Drew's eyes darkened, but he didn't say a word as he turned and stalked away.

CHAPTER 9

I t had finally come. The full moon. Though, of course, it was on a Monday, but Alyssa prepared and took off work Tuesday as she just had a feeling something big was going to happen.

Not forgetting the events from over the weekend, Alyssa tried to keep her nerves at bay. Drew, strangely enough, was off work today, so she quietly got ready for her day to avoid disturbing him. Once she was finished, she debated leaving without waking him to say goodbye, but after their conversation the previous night, she couldn't just leave.

She gently shook his arm. "Baby? I'm going to work now. I'll see you when I get home."

He barely cracked open his eyes and leaned up for a kiss. "Be careful," he mumbled.

"I will."

She walked out the door and hopped in the car for her morning commute.

Arriving early to work, she immediately spotted Jasmine sitting in her chair and made a beeline towards her. "I need to vent," Alyssa said immediately.

"Well, hello. Good morning to you too, sunshine." Jasmine replied with a look. "What's going on? What did he do this time?"

"How do you figure?" Alyssa countered.

Jasmine raised her eyebrows. "Girl, what else do you have going on that you would need to vent about?"

"I have other things in my life, too, you know."

"Sure you do," Jasmine said skeptically. "Now spill."

Alyssa sighed, realizing it's time she told more of the truth about what's been going on and started from the beginning. "This is going to sound crazy, but I need you to listen to me and know I'm not making any of this up."

"You've got me real curious now," Jasmine said, readjusting in her chair.

"Okay. So, you know how we live in this old farmhouse style property with woods all around, right? Well over the past few months, I've been feeling a pull towards them – only on the full moon – and I've been seeing things in there."

"Well, that explains the werewolf conversation from a few weeks ago." Jasmine was quick and never forgot anything Alyssa said. "What have you been seeing?"

"The first time I saw a light. The second time I saw a shadow of a figure."

"That's it? A light and a shadow?" Jasmine raised her eyebrows as Alyssa gave her an exasperated look. "Okay, okay, continue."

"That's the reason Drew and I built the trail with the lights on it. So that I can go figure out what this is. But the thing is, while he was nonchalant about it at first, he's been increasingly against it lately. He's been making comments, mean comments, and just acting weird. He says he's got things on his mind, but he's shutting me out. We had another fight last night." She bit her lip. "I basically told him I was thinking of leaving if he didn't change."

Jasmine's jaw dropped. "Woah, woah, woah. I didn't realize things were that bad."

"Well, I didn't say it just like that, but that's what I think I meant. Whether or not it came through like that, I'm not sure. Part of me hopes it did, while the other part hopes he didn't catch on."

"You can't just say things like that, Alyssa."

"I know. But I meant it. I can't deal with how he's been acting. He's going from hot to cold so quickly that it's giving me whiplash." Alyssa sighed again. "I love him, I truly do. And I know he's going through some things, but if he's going to act like this and shut me out while making me feel like crap at the same time, I'm not going to stand for it."

"I think you two need to sit down and have a legit heart to heart. It seems like something's not clicking right now. He's struggling. You're struggling because of it. Work it out. Or better yet, go to couples therapy."

"I'm sorry, did you just tell me to go to therapy? The woman who doesn't believe in that?" Alyssa exaggerated her shock by pressing her hand to her chest.

"I just want to see you happy." Jasmine ignored Alyssa's comment. "Whether that's fixing your marriage with Drew," she made a face when she said his name, "or moving on to greener pastures, happiness is what I want for you."

Alyssa gave Jasmine a hug. "You're the best, Jazz. Thank you so much."

Jasmine returned the hug. "Now get out of my office, I have work to do," she said with a wink.

The rest of the day passed uneventfully. On the way home Alyssa turned up her radio and tried to put herself in a good mood for Drew. She didn't know what to expect when she walked through the doors, but she knew she wasn't going to be the one starting a fight today.

She walked inside, expecting to see him lounging on the sofa, but surprisingly the TV wasn't even on. She looked around briefly, but didn't see him. "Drew, I'm home," she called, walking towards the bedroom.

Once inside, she began to change into her after work clothes – an old T-shirt and some comfortable shorts. She turned around to throw her clothes into the laundry basket and almost ran right into Drew.

"Drew!" she exclaimed. "I didn't even hear you come in!"

He leaned down to give her a kiss, holding his arm behind his back. "Welcome home, my love."

Her skin pricked and her hair stood on end. Something was wrong. Something was very wrong. She instinctively took a step back, though unsure why. "Drew, are you okay?"

"Never better, baby," he smiled. His smile didn't quite reach his eyes.

She narrowed her eyes at him. "What's behind your back?"

"I wanted to make up for what I said the other day," he began. "So I got you a surprise!" His voice cracked as he brought his arm around to the front of his body.

"Drew…Drew what is that?" She looked at him with fear in her eyes.

"Well clearly a machete," he laughed. She vaguely remembered those same words she spoke not too long ago, but in an entirely different context. "Wait. I have a better idea."

She took a step back as he put the shining machete down and let out a nervous laughter. "Drew, what's going on?" He stared at her, something abnormal in his eyes. Her eyes darted for an escape, but the only way out was past him and there was no way she could get by without him grabbing her. She had to try. She bolted towards the door, as far away from him as she could, but it was no use. He grabbed her arm and pulled her close.

"Where are you going?" he breathed into her ear.

"Drew, stop this, please! I don't know what I did, but I'm sorry!" she cried out, tears starting to slide down her cheeks. "Drew!" She struggled, but his grip on her wrist was too tight. It was going to leave bruises for sure.

He slid his free hand up her body. She froze, a familiar feeling creeping back. A memory she suppressed from long ago. She knew where this was headed, but didn't understand why. "Drew," she whispered. "Please, don't do this. Not like this." A new wave of fear erupted inside of her as she felt his hand under her shirt, trailing along her bare flesh. She had to reason with him. She had to snap him out of this...whatever it was. "Drew. Baby. What do you want?"

"You. Forever." His voice thick with desire? Longing? She couldn't quite place it. He roughly grabbed her breast as he twisted her wrist behind her back. She grimaced in pain.

"Baby, I've always told you that I'm yours forever." She gritted her teeth. "Not even death could tear us apart." Terrified at the words coming out of her mouth, she knew it was a lie. She had to get away and get away fast.

He nuzzled the back of her head, breathing in the scent of her hair. "Not even death," he murmured into her neck.

"That's right, I'm yours, remember? Please, please stop this and let go of me." She bit her lip hoping he would give in to her pleas.

He released her breast and took his hand out from under her shirt. She tried not to breathe a sigh of relief, though he still had the too tight grip on her wrist behind her back.

His head never left her neck as if he was drinking her in. "Not even death," he repeated.

"Babe?"

His hand trailed up her body again, this time over her shirt, his touch barely there. Her breath caught in her throat. She wanted to scream. She wanted to run. She wanted to get away, but stood paralyzed with fear.

Suddenly he grabbed her neck and pulled her against him. His grip tightened on both her wrist and her neck. Panic broke out and she began flailing with her free hand and kicking backwards.

He maneuvered towards the bed and shoved her down, letting go of her throbbing wrist, but with his hand still on her neck. Her face began turning red. She thrashed, hoping to make contact and be released from his grip, but it was as if each blow bounced right off him. What was going on? Surely she wasn't that weak.

She started seeing stars, but continued to thrash. Suddenly the grip on her neck loosened. She gasped for breath and went to scream, but his grip tightened again, cutting her scream and oxygen off. He ripped at her shorts and underwear, exposing her. *This can't be happening*, she thought and thrashed again. He simply ignored her and took off his pants. She began to scratch at his arm holding her down, leaving slightly bloody trails down his forearm.

Her head was suddenly knocked to the side as he slapped her across the face hard. "Fucking bitch." She started to see stars again, her face a deep red now. "If you fucking scream, I'll kill you." He carefully released his grip on her neck and she gasped for air once more. Once her face turned a bright cherry color, no longer the dark red it was, he tightened his grip again, placing the other hand on her neck as well. Tears flowed down her cheeks as the dark image of her once loving husband blocked the bedroom from view.

He abruptly thrust inside her. She opened her mouth to scream in pain, but nothing came out. She started to see stars again and the edges of her vision started to blacken. Her thrashing slowed as her vision darkened while he relentlessly continued thrusting inside her. He released his grip, but held her shoulders down.

"Stop," she croaked out between gasps. Her throat was on fire, her face throbbed, her body was screaming in agony. Wasn't adrenaline supposed to suppress this pain? She tried once more to gather what strength she had left and kick him off, but it didn't work. He grabbed her neck and slapped her again, enjoying seeing her tear-stained face in distress as the red mark slowly spread across her cheek.

Now that she was able to breathe, Alyssa began to sob as his assault continued. "Drew. Drew, please." Her voice didn't sound like her own and she didn't understand why he was doing any of this.

"Shut up!" He placed both hands on her neck and squeezed again, thrusting faster and harder into her. He squeezed harder, enjoying the sensation of her body squirming under his. His ecstasy took over as he stopped thinking, only reacting. He looked up and closed his eyes, gritting his teeth, hands still tightly wrapped around his wife's neck. He felt it. He was close. Her squirming slowed and he looked down at her face. There's that deep purple again. This time, he didn't release her neck, but held on, not even feeling the fading scratching of her nails against his exposed arm. He was almost there, just a little bit more. Her body started going limp, her face a deeper, darker purple. He finished just as she passed out, groaning in ecstasy as his wife lay limp beneath him. He sat there a few seconds longer with his hands still around her throat. Releasing her, he knew he would certainly kill her if he persisted.

Her body began to breathe again. A wicked idea crossed his mind as he watched his wife of five years lay bruised and broken in their bed.

CHAPTER 10

Alyssa awoke, throat on fire, body screaming, head throbbing. She tried to move her arms, but found herself bound. *No!* She struggled and pulled at the restraints, trying to see if there were any weak spot she could break free from. Her legs were left unbound. She twisted her body, trying to break free, but only wound up hurting herself more. She began sobbing as she looked around for Drew. *This can't be happening. This can't be happening.* She kept repeating that thought in her head.

She turned and looked at the restraints through tear-filled eyes – a thick nylon rope. Stretching her fingers, she attempted scratching at them, knowing it was useless. *Why? Why is he doing this?* She sobbed harder, not realizing the sounds of her anguish attracted the attention of her captor.

"You're awake!" He said brightly, walking into the room towards her, a glass of clear liquid in his hands. "Here, drink this." She shut her lips, turning her head away from him. He grabbed her hair and yanked her heads towards him. She gasped in pain. "I said drink this you fucking bitch."

Her lips trembled as she weighed her options. "What...what is it?" she croaked out, trying to stall.

"Water. I'm sure you're thirsty," the tone of his voice switching back and forth rapidly.

"No. I'm not," she managed to get out, moving her restrained body as far as she could away from him.

He grabbed her jaw too hard. "I. Said. Drink!" He forced her mouth open and poured water inside, causing her to choke. "See, now look what you did." He held her head in place as she struggled, water spraying out with each cough. He clicked his tongue, stood up, releasing her head.

She immediately turned her head to the side, still coughing. She didn't think it was possible for her throat to burn worse. "Please. Please just let me go. I won't run, I won't scream, I won't say anything," she began sobbing again. "Just please let me go."

He began pacing. "You're the one that wanted forever, remember?" Her bruised face paled at the memory.

"Is that what started this? That one...that one comment?" She struggled to talk.

He ignored her, still pacing.

"Drew. Answer me. Is that it?"

He walked up to her and slapped her again as she cried out in pain. "You're in no position for demands, my love." He sat next to her, facing away.

She sobbed again, futilely scratching at the rope around her wrists. She didn't even notice that he had fully unclothed her. He turned to her, grabbing a fistful of hair, and aggressively kissed her. She gasped, allowing his tongue to enter her mouth. She bit down as she kicked towards him, knowing full well what was next. He yelped and pulled back as his hand swung. Her cheeks were starting to go numb now.

"Fucking whore." He grabbed her hair once more, yanking her head back, and quickly moved his mouth to her breast. He bit down hard, causing her to scream in pain. "You like that?" He moved to the other breast and did the same. "I'll fucking break you," he said just before biting her. She screamed again. He raised up and kissed her again. Once again, she refused him. He pulled away, keeping his hand tangled in her hair. "That's how it's going to be? You're rejecting your husband?"

"You're not my husband like this," she spat.

"That hurts. Truly it does. If that's how you feel, let's have some real fun now." He lifted her by the hair and slammed her head against the headboard. She saw stars again. "Look what you made me do." He released her and kissed her forehead, causing her to shudder. He trailed soft, gentle kisses down her exposed body, stopping at her most sensitive part. He began exploring her with his tongue.

"You're disgusting," she cried out, kicking her legs around.

He stopped, grabbed her legs, and sat on top of them. He gently put two fingers inside her and began softly thrusting them in and out. "Still dry. Let's change that." He rearranged to lay on top of her, his body away from her legs and face over her crotch.

She kicked, but with how his body was positioned, she was just kicking air. His weight felt crushing. She suddenly felt a warm sensation as he began exploring her again with his tongue. "No!" she shouted, struggling against his weight and the restraints. Her breathing quickened as her body realized it wasn't getting enough air as she was only able to take shallow breaths. She felt a panic attack coming on. She felt suffocated again. "Drew!" she screamed out, gasping for breath, her body still trying to shake him off.

Whether he mistook her reaction as pleasure or he simply didn't care, he smiled and licked his two fingers, aggressively shoving them inside her again. His tongue continued its assault on her as his fingers thrusted in and out. She began hyperventilating as she started to get lightheaded. He forced his legs under and around the back of her head, crossing them, pushing her head up, making it even harder for her to breathe. "Drew…" she weakly called out between gasps. Hearing her struggle, he pushed his weight down on her, still going at it. She felt him through his pants; his erect penis pressing hard into her chest. He pulled his fingers out, examining them as he continued with his tongue.

He suddenly stopped and rolled off her, taking off his pants. "You like that, baby?" He asked as she gasped, finally able to take a deep breath.

"Fuck you," she managed to get out.

"Oh, I plan on it." He smirked and got on top of her. He thrust into her so hard she screamed. She swore she felt something tear. "Isn't this what you wanted? You said fuck me!" he said between grunts. She began crying in pain again. Annoyed with her constant noises, he put his hands around her neck again. "It's time for you to shut up." He squeezed as her eyes went wide in realization.

Unable to do anything, but barely squirm her body, she couldn't fight back this time. He loved the fear in her eyes. He loved the changing colors of her face. He loved the way his hands wrapped perfectly around her delicate throat. But most of all, he loved how she felt. Her squirming body messed with his rhythm, but her struggling caused her to clench around him, tightening her grip, driving him insane with desire.

Her squirming slowed and he released her neck. "Hey now. You're not finished, yet. Don't you pass out on me."

She involuntarily gasped for breath again. She wished she would just die. Why did he have to torture her like this. Just let her pass out and finish the job. How long would this go on?

He continued thrusting as the red in her face faded. He looked at her face, cheeks now covered in blackening bruises. A face that would once get him off with just a look, now isn't doing it for him. He needed more. "Scream for me, baby," he pleaded, throwing his head back and closing his eyes.

Dizzy, she didn't quite comprehend what he wanted. She began to loudly fake moan, thinking that's what he needed to hear. Anything to get this to stop.

His head shot forward and his eyes flew open. "You lying cunt. I told you before to never fake on me!" He grabbed her neck again, squeezing harder than before. She struggled against him, which only seemed to make him thrust faster. "Yes, keep struggling, baby!" He threw his head back in ecstasy as her body slowed. Her vision started fading and she silently prayed this was the end. No such luck. He released and her body gasped again.

How much more of this could she take? Her ears were ringing. Her chest and throat were on fire. Her head was spinning so much she thought she would vomit. She somehow kept it down, knowing this sick bastard would probably let her choke on it.

Drew's high faded as he looked down at the broken woman beneath him. He continued thrusting, but without the same vigor as before. He needed to get off and he needed it now, but it was disappearing. He didn't think, just reacted, as he grabbed her nipples with both hands and twisted hard. She screamed in pain again, which seemed to fuel his frenzy. He leaned into her and kissed her open mouth, hands still violently twisting her nipples. She turned her head away from him, struggling once more to try to get away.

Enraged at her refusal of him again, he released her nipples and grabbed her neck again. "Bitch!" he cried out, squeezing again. Her face quickly turned red, then darker red, then purple. He felt it again. His pleasure rising. He threw his head back, continuing to choke the life out of her. Her face was now that familiar purple color and her vision started going black again. He leaned down to kiss her once more, not releasing his grip, this time not caring that she didn't or couldn't kiss back. She stopped squirming now and her eyes slowly closed. He loved the color of her skin. He held his grip, thrusting over and over, getting closer and closer. It wouldn't come. "Fucking bitch can't even do your job right," he spat out towards the unresponsive body underneath him. He never let go of her throat, using her as leverage to thrust deeper and deeper.

He had never been so deep in. Even as she slept, nothing felt this good. He kept going, feeling the blossoming orgasm creeping up on him. Pleasure taking over, he tightened his loosened grip on her throat, fingernails digging into her flesh, continuing his hard, fast assault on her unconscious body. He glanced down once more at the beautiful face, now an array of dark colors. It finally hit. His body exploded into pleasure as he screamed out. He felt the throbbing continue as he finally stopped thrusting. Sweat dripping from his forehead and eyes still closed, he breathed hard, never experiencing an orgasm like that before in his life.

He slowly opened his eyes, hands still gripping Alyssa's throat. He released his grip and stretched his stiff fingers. He pulled out of her and flopped on the bed next to her, her body still. "You're amazing," he said to her, not looking at her. He closed his eyes, exhausted, and quickly fell asleep next to his wife.

Chapter 11

Opening his eyes, Drew stretched and rolled over, glancing over at the corpse of his young wife laying lifelessly next to him. "Good morning, beautiful," he said to her, with a small smile.

Of course, there was no reply.

Recalling the events from the night before, Drew didn't feel any remorse. He stood up and sighed heavily, unsure of his next step. He had been fired from his job the week prior, though he hadn't told Alyssa and given her comment from the other night, he was glad he didn't say anything.

She claimed she wanted forever, but then was thinking of leaving? He couldn't let that happen.

He walked to the kitchen to make a cup of coffee and toss some frozen sausage in a pan. As he was cooking, he thought about how amazing last night felt and a deranged smile crept up on his face. Once breakfast was finished, he sat on the sofa and turned on the TV - not really watching, but lost in his own thoughts.

Alyssa and her family don't speak that often and aren't really close, so ignoring any potential phone calls from them shouldn't be an issue. But what about her work? She took off Tuesday, so they won't be looking for her then, but Wednesday? He knew she was close with some of her coworkers. He would just tell them she was terribly sick.

Now what about the body? He couldn't bear the thought of getting rid of it. Not when she had just become perfect. "She's mine and isn't going anywhere," he said aloud.

With that he turned his full attention to the TV. Once bored with the shows, he got up and put his dirty dishes in the dishwasher, which still held clean dishes from the night before. Briefly contemplating putting them up or letting Alyssa handle them, he realized that this was all on him. "Oh, right," he said to no one. Removing the clean dishes, he worked on chores like normal.

He noticed the electric bill on the counter. They had some savings, so he didn't need to find a job right away. Plus, he had her credit cards. He could run them up as it didn't matter anymore. What would Alyssa want him to do?

The answer was obvious, find a job. So, he sighed and pulled out a laptop to search for jobs. He browsed job listings with no real interest and quickly got bored.

His thoughts took over again as he stared blankly at the screen. He felt an odd sense of freedom, as though the rest of the world was irrelevant. Despite this freedom, a weight began to press against his chest.

He glanced back to the bedroom. Alyssa's face, so full of fear in her last moments, popped into his mind, instantly making him excited again. She deserved what she got. If she was really planning on leaving and was set on that path, he just made it faster.

He turned his attention back to the laptop, determined to find something to occupy his time. He clicked a few posts, but was easily distracted by the thought of the beauty lying in their bed. He could almost hear her voice in his head urging him to find something to make him happy. Well, now he had. He had everything he ever wanted. Freedom; a sense of control; the life he dreamed of.

A noise in the hallway jolted him from his thoughts. He quickly turned to look, but saw nothing. He got up to investigate and saw that a photo of them had fallen and shattered glass was scattered across the tile floor. Barefoot, he grumbled about having to clean up the mess. He grabbed some shoes and the broom, sweeping up the shards of glass. Once that was cleared, he picked up their photo and the frame. Unsure of why it had fallen, his mind told him the universe knew what he had done. He huffed at the ridiculous thought and placed them on the coffee table in the living room.

Walking back to their bedroom, he took in her form, still laying in the same position he left her in this morning. Arms still tied to the bedposts, bruises on her neck, a strange color creeping over her skin. Though he enjoyed seeing her in that position, he felt as though it would be uncomfortable for a long period of time. He untied her bindings and tried to move her limbs, but realized rigor mortis had set in.

Frustrated, he decided to wait it out before readjusting her. He placed a blanket on her exposed body up to her chin. "There. You're safe now," he murmured.

He felt content at his good deed and decided to head back to the living room with a new sense of purpose. He decided to find a job and live a life as normal as possible to ensure there were no questions, no interruptions. He couldn't bear to lose her twice.

After a few hours of playing on the computer – a mixture of job hunting and browsing social media – he decided it was time for lunch. He opened the refrigerator, looking for some sort of leftovers as he didn't have the energy to cook. Finding nothing of interest, he decided on a pack of instant noodles and put a pot of water on the stove to boil.

Once he was finished with lunch, he went back into the bedroom. He smiled each time he saw his quiet, obedient wife.

He didn't realize how much she talked. How much she bothered him. Not until now when all was silent. He walked back out and decided to take a nap on the sofa. He dreamed of amazing sex and a quiet wife.

A chill crept up on him, causing him to open his eyes. Something wasn't right. The air around him felt heavier and it was cold in their normally warm house.

Getting up to investigate, Drew felt another chill creep up his spine. He immediately went into the bedroom to grab the handgun he kept in the nightstand drawer. The air somehow felt even colder in here. He briefly glanced at his wife and noticed the blanket had shifted. He paused, furrowing his brow in confusion.

Suddenly, Alyssa's hand twitched, causing Drew to jump back. "A-Alyssa?" he whispered.

A low groan escaped her lips.

This can't be happening, he thought to himself. It must have been a trick of the mind. He continued staring at her, forgetting the chill in the air.

Her eyes snapped open as she turned them to look at him, not moving her head. He gasped, panic surging through him. She started moving her stiff body. He backed up, fear racing in his heart.

"Drew..." she muttered out, barely comprehensible.

Did she remember what happened or is she just looking for him for comfort? Drew's mind was racing with questions, mainly *How is this possible?*

She shifted her body to get off the bed and stand. Frozen with fear, all Drew could do was watch as his wife's reanimated corpse staggered towards him.

He looked at her eyes, once filled with warmth and love, replaced by a deep fear last night; they were emotionless and dead now. Her body jerked, her movements stiff and unnatural. She stumbled towards him while he stood there, still frozen in awe and fear.

His breath hitched in his throat as she got within arm's reach of him. He instinctively took a step back as she took another step forward. She reached her arm towards him and placed it on his chest. He held his breath, unsure of her next move. Her eyes, unwavering, never left his. Had she always had this intense of a gaze?

Suddenly, her hand plunged into his chest, tearing through flesh and breaking bones. Her hand gripped his heart as he screamed in agony.

Drew jolted up, covered in sweat and gasping for air. His hand instinctively went to his chest – no hole and he felt his heart pounding. He took in his surroundings, extremely confused. He was on the sofa in the living room. *A dream*, he thought. Rather, a nightmare. He stood up and walked to the bedroom.

Alyssa lay just as he left her, blanket in place. He released a breath he didn't know he had been holding.

"How ridiculous," he muttered to himself. "I can't believe I thought that was real." He shook his head at his foolishness and turned his back to the body lying in the bed. He didn't notice her eyes slightly move under her eyelids.

CHAPTER 12

The moon illuminated the property as a will-o'-the-wisp floated carelessly throughout the trees. A mist-like figure formed in Drew and Alyssa's bedroom. It was roughly the size of an adult, somehow swirling while keeping its form.

Alyssa looked down at her body covered up by the blanket. She noticed the bruises on her neck and wrists as anger welled up inside her. Something shining just at the edge of the blanket caught her attention. She moved to see what it was, curious. It was her necklace with the red jeweled pendant Drew had given her.

Her face crunched up in anger; she wanted revenge. She tried moving the blanket to cover more of her bruises, but realized she didn't have a physical body to touch anything.

Frustrated, she let out a scream, audible only to her own ears. "That bastard," she said to herself. "I'll kill him," she vowed as she floated out of the bedroom, looking for him.

As she expected, he was on the sofa watching TV. Did he do anything else? Quickly floating towards him, she tried punching him, only to phase right through him. He did blink, however, though whether it was coincidence or something she did, she wasn't sure.

She screamed in frustration again and began float-pacing, her thoughts racing. She realized she was dead. So that would make her a ghost now. But why did she just appear? Shouldn't she have jumped into the spirit world the moment the life left her physical body? She shook her head, unable to fully comprehend what was happening.

Infuriated, she tried hitting Drew again, only to phase through him once more. Realizing her predicament, she gave up, even more frustrated than before.

She floated out of the house, away from her once-husband. Something caught her eye towards the woods. *Is it that a light?* she thought to herself.

Quickly heading towards the woods, the light stayed, as if waiting for her. Once she got there, she stopped and took in exactly what it was. An orb of ice-blue light, dancing in small movements. It ventured into the woods and of course, Alyssa followed, hoping to finally get her answers.

She no longer felt the pull she had been feeling for months. She guessed that feeling left when she had died. Following the light, she did not stay on the path, instead phased through trees farther to the left of where she and Drew had spent days perfecting her vision.

After floating along for several minutes, the orb stopped over a small clearing. Alyssa took in their surroundings, illuminated by the moon through the openings of the trees. There were small saplings growing in this clearing along with mushrooms in a circle. An odd sight, given that the mushrooms in these woods typically grew on rotting wood.

A mist swirled above the circle of mushrooms, taking the shape of a woman without a face. Alyssa gasped and floated backwards slightly, forgetting she was mist now as well.

"I've been watching you," a gentle female voice emerged from the newly formed figure. "I was trying to warn you."

"What are you talking about?" Alyssa asked, confused. "Wait, I can hear you. Can you hear me?"

"Yes, we're in the same plane now," the faceless figure replied. "I was hoping to save you from the same fate."

"The same fate…" Alyssa trailed off then repeated, "What are you talking about?"

"Did he ever tell you he was married once before?"

"What?!" Alyssa exclaimed.

"I figured not. My story isn't that different from yours, sadly." The figure sighed.

"What are you saying? Stop being so cryptic!" Alyssa was already frustrated and couldn't help but lash out at the strange figure that seemed to be withholding information.

"My name was Lily and I was Drew's first wife." Alyssa gasped as the figure continued. "I was deeply, madly in love with Drew. He was everything I ever wanted. Sweet, caring, fun, loving, made me laugh, you know the typical Prince Charming."

Alyssa kept silent, listening intently to Lily's story.

"He started changing. It was slight at first, but he went downhill pretty quickly. He claimed he had a lot on his mind."

Gee, that sounds familiar, Alyssa thought.

"One night, he completely lost it and attacked me. He wound up stabbing me so…many…times. The pain was indescribable. At the end, I was grateful for death." Alyssa felt a pain in her chest as Lily's story sounded similar to her own. "I don't exactly remember what happened next, but I remember seeing him doing horrendous things to my body. I was furious. I wanted revenge. But I couldn't seem to manifest myself to get it. After a while, I think he panicked. People were starting to question where I was and he could only put it off for so long. He dragged my body out to this spot and buried me deep. I don't know how he dug such a hole, but he dropped my body inside, covered me up with dirt like I was nothing, then put our dog that he had also killed above me. I guess to throw off any cadaver dogs that would have come searching."

"That's horrible," Alyssa whispered.

"That pendant," she vaguely gestured in Alyssa's direction. "That used to be mine. I'm so sorry that I couldn't save you. He's a despicable human being who doesn't deserve life." Lily sounded as if she were going to cry.

"So, you were the light I kept seeing. Were you trying to call me here to tell me?"

"Yes. I didn't know if it would work, since it's been so long since I've tried communicating with anyone, but I had to try."

Alyssa's mind was racing. Drew being married once before, talking to a ghost, being a ghost herself, seeing her body, and now knowing her body's fate that lie ahead in the upcoming days. It was too much. If she were alive, she may have passed out.

"What can we do?" she asked weakly.

"Nothing. I haven't been able to do anything," Lily spat out. "I've been stuck here, watching the same events unfold that happened years ago."

"How long ago did this happen?" Alyssa asked gently, needing to know.

"About five years ago."

Five years, Alyssa thought. That was right when she and Drew had started dating. Thinking back, she didn't notice anything off with him. Did she just miss the signs?

As if reading her thoughts, Lily piped up, "You couldn't have known. He was, and still is, a master liar. I don't understand how he did it, but he appeared as if he had no remorse. Hell, he must not have had any remorse, given what he did to my body after. I have a sneaking suspicion that you'll be going through the same thing as me.

My advice? Do not go into that house. You don't want to see what I saw."

The realization of what Lily was telling her finally dawned on Alyssa. Despicable doesn't even begin to describe Drew. She had to exact her revenge, for both her and Lily. But how? If Lily was unsuccessful for the past five years, how could Alyssa expect to do anything having just died? But she couldn't let Drew hurt anyone else.

Lily floated in silence as Alyssa's thoughts and emotions swirled as much as the mist creating her figure did.

"Lily?" Alyssa began softly. "I'm so sorry. I'm sorry for both of us. But I have more questions. Why did you only start appearing recently? How did you make me feel what I did? Why only on the full moon?"

"I still don't quite understand everything myself. After I realized there was nothing I could do, I accepted that I was destined to roam these woods alone. I had hoped there was a moving on process for me, but nothing ever happened. As far as why only recently, well, I didn't know what I could do. I tried coming to you when you were alone, you just never seemed to notice me. I think maybe your instincts kicked in the harder I tried. As if your soul knew something was wrong. Once I started seeing the signs in him, I had to try even harder. That's when I had the idea to try to catch your attention with a light; so I transformed myself into an orb and floated along the tree line. I knew Drew would be uncomfortable coming back in here, which is why I insisted on the woods."

"But why the full moon? Why just once a month? Things might have been different if you had told me sooner!" Alyssa was getting emotional again.

"The full moon is when I feel the most powerful. I tried other nights, but couldn't quite shift into the orb. I don't understand that part either. Remember, I quit trying and wandered for years, sinking into only what I can describe as a depression. Can ghosts even get depressed?" She gave a half-hearted laugh.

Alyssa didn't find this situation funny at all. Instead, she grew even more heated, feeling the red-hot anger boiling in her chest. She looked up at the treetops and screamed again. This time, the sound echoed around them.

Lily stood silently shocked. "Alyssa...do you realize what you just did?"

Panting, Alyssa felt slightly better, but glanced at the faceless Lily.

"You made a sound! A real sound!"

Confused, Alyssa paused. "I did?"

"Your blood was probably boiling too loudly to hear it, but you echoed throughout the woods!" Lily got excited now. "Maybe you can make a difference! The difference I wasn't able to make! Maybe you can stop him for good this time."

Alyssa thought for a minute. "If you couldn't do it in fve years, what makes you think I can do anything after just one scream and having just died?"

"You're different, Alyssa. You and I were cut from a different cloth. I was always more timid and you seem strong-willed and determined. I really think your spirit is stronger than mine had ever been and will ever be."

"Okay, how do we do this?" Alyssa asked, the anger calming down slightly, her mind racing with possibilities.

"That's up to you," Lily said. "This is your show. Run it."

"Won't you help me?"

"I've done all I can do. I think it's time for me to rest now." With that, Lily faded away, leaving Alyssa floating alone in the woods.

CHAPTER 13

Drew walked out to the front porch leaving the light off, beer in hand, and sat down in his chair. The light from the moon bounced off both of their vehicles. He stared at Alyssa's car. Thinking of her absurd obsession with the full moon and the woods, he rolled his eyes.

"At least that's over with," he said to no one as he took a sip of his beer. His mind wandered to the once cleared spot in the woods and what lay beneath. He was careful to lead Alyssa away from that area when building her senseless path.

He could have built the path leading directly to that spot and she would have been none the wiser, but he didn't want to take that risk. He wanted to keep her in the dark of his deepest secrets.

Truth be told he wasn't thinking about his career these past few months. What had truly been on his mind lately was that troublesome first wife of his. He tried pushing her out of his mind, but she continued haunting him. He swore he even saw her around the property a couple of times, though he knew that was impossible.

Why did she have to ruin what he had? Things were going great between him and Alyssa, but she had to creep into his mind and not let go like the crazy ex she was. His predicament was her fault.

Drew took another sip of his beer, the bitter taste mixing well with the bitterness of his thoughts. Leaning back in his chair, he glanced at the moonlit sky, the cicadas' song echoing throughout the nearby woods. The air felt heavy.

Alyssa's smiling face appeared in his thoughts, her laughter echoing throughout his mind. He then thought to her state just inside in their bedroom and the dream he had earlier that day. A chill crept up his spine. Suddenly feeling watched, he quickly went inside.

He locked the door and glanced towards the bedroom. Though he knew it was irrational, he decided to ensure her body was where he left it. He held his breath as he crossed the threshold expecting to see her standing up, ready to rip his heart out. Breathing a sigh of relief, he saw she was still under the blanket, unmoving.

Taking this opportunity to admire her once more, he pulled back the blanket, exposing her unclothed multicolored body. A serene smile appeared in his face. "Mine," he whispered as he brushed the back of his hand against her cold cheek. "Mine forever."

He was too entranced to notice the chill in the air. Too wrapped up in his own sick thoughts to feel the tingling in his spine.

Though she was told to stay out of the house, Alyssa couldn't stand by and let her body be violated again. Feeling the rage build in her chest again, she screamed.

Hearing the scream, Drew jumped back and instinctively turned around, his eyes darting around. He saw nothing. He backed up towards the bed, finally feeling the change in the air surrounding him.

"Alyssa?!" he called, thinking he recognized her voice through the gut-wrenching noise. He thought it was impossible. No, he knew it was impossible. This must be another dream. He breathed a sigh of relief, realizing that he must have fallen asleep.

Drew turned back to his wife's corpse as Alyssa charged at him, trying to get him away from her body. She phased through him; he felt a jolt of electricity and paused, spine still tingling.

"Get away from me!" she yelled, though it didn't seem as if he heard her. He shrugged and ran his fingers through her hair. He grew excited as he took off his pants, staring at her lifeless face.

Alyssa couldn't take anymore and screamed again. Drew snapped his head around, clearly hearing her again. Feeling uneasy, he put his pants back on and grabbed his handgun from the nightstand. He searched every room in the house then grabbed a spotlight and headed outside.

"This is just a dream," he kept repeating, as if trying to comfort himself. He shined the light everywhere, carefully checking around the house, in the shed, and between their vehicles. His search came up empty.

Alyssa was following him around, trying to push him down, to punch him, anything. How did he feel her before? Heading back inside, he paused on the porch. She took this opportunity to try to tackle him down the steps. She flew at him as quickly as she could, phasing through him again, causing another jolt of electricity to shoot through his body. He instinctively took a step back, his foot slipping off the porch, causing him to lose his balance and fall down the 4 steps onto the gravel below.

Feeling accomplished, Alyssa floated down to see the damage. "Damn," she said. He was still alive.

He groaned and looked down at his leg, fully expecting it to be broken given the pain he was in. To his surprise, everything was intact. "Must be a sprain," he muttered. He gingerly stood up, not putting pressure on that leg. He brushed the gravel that was stuck to his skin off. His arms and legs burned where the sharp rocks had cut into him.

Looking up at the porch, he wondered how he was going to get inside. Deciding to take the easy way, he hopped to the porch and sat down on one of the steps. Using his arms and good leg, he pulled himself backwards up the steps, knowing full well if he tried going up the steps normally, he would fall and cause more damage.

Alyssa floated by his side, seething at her failure, the accomplished feeling from before long gone. She tried kicking him, but her foot phased through him, just as before.

Drew didn't notice the small jolts of electricity shooting through him, the pain from his leg and the burning in his arms overshadowing it. He used the doorknob as leverage as he pulled himself up. Hopping inside, he shut the door behind him. He hobbled to the freezer grabbed an ice pack.

"Sure could use her right now," he mumbled, realizing he was on his own to treat himself. He limped over to the sofa and sat down heavily. He lifted his leg and gently pressed the ice pack against his ankle. He winced in pain. "How did I even manage that?" he grumbled to himself, replaying the scene from moments before.

He had felt the electricity again. The screams, the chill in the air, the electric shocks, he tried putting the pieces together. He hadn't seen anything, but it started when he was in the room with Alyssa. "Maybe it was her ghost," he said cynically. "She's out for revenge." He let out a small laugh. "I don't know what she could be unhappy with! I just gave her what she wanted. She should be thanking me, not pushing me down the stairs!"

Alyssa fumed, realizing he still didn't think he did anything wrong. She wished she would have broken his back, causing him to lay there, suffering and alone until he died.

Spiraling down, Drew called out to her. "You were supposed to be here to take care of me! Now look what you've done. I'm alone and in pain because of you," he spat out.

Wishing she could reanimate her body, Alyssa envisioned herself clawing Drew to death.

Drew couldn't shake the feeling that he wasn't alone. He felt her presence. He knew she was there. "I know you're here, Alyssa! Don't be a coward! Show yourself!" he shouted to the empty air.

How she wished she could do just that. She floated in front of him and focused, trying to manifest herself into the physical realm. The best she got was a slight mist, though she doubted he would notice – if he could even see her. "I'm right here, you bastard!" she shouted, but he didn't react.

Drew grumbled again, the late night and his heavy thoughts catching up with him. He lay on the sofa and carefully balanced the ice pack on his leg, hoping to go to sleep. Realizing he should probably take a pain killer before bed, he groaned and stood up to hop towards the bedroom.

Alyssa took this opportunity to try to knock him down again. She flew at his back, phasing through him. He felt the jolt once more, but kept his balance this time. Limping past the bed, he made it to the bathroom and grabbed three pain pills. Alyssa floated right behind him, rage coursing through her misty body.

She looked in the mirror and shockingly saw herself. A translucent body with wild, floating hair. A wicked smile filled her face. She gathered her strength and screamed again, causing Drew to look up in the mirror. His face paled at what he saw looking back at him.

He spun around, but saw nothing. He looked back at the mirror again to see the ethereal face of his dead wife staring back at him with a maniacal smile. He screamed and fell backwards, forgetting the pain in his leg. Scrambling to place his back against the wall, he frantically looked around. "Alyssa?" he called wildly, eyes scanning the bathroom trying to find the figure he just saw.

She was enjoying this. His fear, his panic; it was delicious. She slowly floated in front of Drew, who was close to hyperventilating. She focused all her energy on manifesting once again, hoping to appear in more than just a mirror. She watched him carefully, examining him for any indication that he could see her.

His eyes still frantically searched the bathroom, fear gripping his heart. Directly in front of him, a mist began swirling. His breath caught in his throat. "No, no, no," Drew realized what was happening, though his brain couldn't quite comprehend how it was possible.

Alyssa's figure formed as he looked up at her in fear. Her hair floated around her wildly; her eyes, no longer the warm and loving sight he was used to, now held an unimaginable coldness to them. She reached her hand toward him as he screamed. He scrambled out of the door as she smiled. She was starting to have way too much fun.

Following him, she laughed as he hobbled throughout the house. Where was he going to go? There was nowhere she couldn't follow him. She felt her energy draining. "No, not now!" she cried. Just as she had caught his attention her figure flickered and faded away.

Drew stopped at the kitchen, grabbed a knife from the block, and sat down against a wall in the corner, panting. He looked around, but didn't see anything. Not daring to move, he held his breath, trying to hear over his pounding heart. Silence greeted him. He didn't see any figures, didn't hear any screams, didn't feel any electric shocks. *She couldn't be gone,* he thought. No, she was too stubborn to leave once she got somewhere she wanted to be. Or maybe he imagined the entire thing.

Alyssa floated by him, watching him, seething at her own incompetence to keep her form. Forgetting that she had been dead for barely over a day, she was frustrated she couldn't hold the manifestation for longer. She should be proud of herself, accomplishing something that Lily couldn't in her five years in the spirit world. But there was nothing to be proud of when the man who killed her still walked the earth.

CHAPTER 14

D rew woke with a start, his body cold and aching from sleeping in an upright position on the floor all night. The previous night's events came rushing back and he quickly grabbed the knife that had fallen next to him. He looked around, staying silent; he didn't see or hear anything.

"Maybe it was a dream," he whispered to himself. Feeling the throb of his leg, he knew deep down that it was real. Impossible, but real. He took a breath, trying to steady his racing heart as he rose to his feet, wincing at the pain coursing through his body.

Though he didn't know what time it was, morning sunlight shone through the curtains. He glanced around, expecting to see her figure watching him from the corner. "Just a dream," he muttered again, though the chill in the air and lingering fear in his chest said otherwise.

He slowly made his way to the coffee machine and fixed a cup, hoping the hot liquid would soothe the aching in his bones. Sitting at a barstool, he watched the steam rising from the mug, mimicking the swirling of Alyssa's figure from the night before. He suddenly pushed the mug away, not wanting it after making the correlation.

He couldn't ignore it anymore. He had to get rid of the body. As much as he didn't want to lose her, too many strange things had happened yesterday. His thoughts raced as he calculated his next move. They didn't have a dog he could bury on top of her, so he had to come up with another plan. He could bury her body in the clearing by the bench. "How bittersweet," he said aloud with a smirk.

That could work. He could then plant flowers throughout the edges of the path, leading up to a sanctuary of plants at the clearing, surrounding the bench. He grinned and grabbed his keys, forgetting how disheveled he looked from the night before.

He limped to his car and realized how much of a challenge driving was going to be. Luckily he didn't injure his driving foot, otherwise this would have proven to be extremely difficult. He carefully drove to the local hardware store and bought all sorts of shrubs and flowers – things that would make sense to Alyssa.

As he was driving back with his truck bed full of plants, he let his mind wander and planned out his next move. He knew she had been posting their progress with the path on social media. To make things less suspicious, he planned on taking a picture of the plants and posting them under her profile.

When he arrived home, he drove to the edge of the woods, pausing to implement the next part of his plan after he parked. He snapped a picture of the plants in the truck bed and, knowing all her passwords, logged into her account, posting them with the caption "Part 2!" Satisfied, he put his phone away and began slowly unloading the plants.

Once everything was unloaded, he drove back to the house and went inside to take some more pain killers, careful to avoid looking at his wife's discolored body in the bedroom. He looked down and away from the mirror, ensuring that he wouldn't see a ghostly face staring back at him.

Limping to the kitchen, he grabbed another ice pack and walked to the sofa. Should his next step be to hide the body or to plant the plants? Either one was going to be difficult in his current state. He could load the body in his truck bed and drive across the yard that night, but digging a large enough hole was the issue. It was enough of a challenge five years ago when he wasn't injured.

He decided to plant what he bought and start digging the hole tonight and fight through the pain. But why wait until tonight? It wasn't like they had neighbors to hide from. Even if they did have neighbors, it would just look like he's working on the path.

After the ice pack mostly thawed and the pain killers kicked in, he decided to head into the woods. Driving his truck to the shed, he grabbed a shovel and a rake the tossed them in the truck bed. He drove to the beginning of the trail. Putting his truck in park and shutting it off, he stared at the daunting woods in front of him.

He slowly grabbed one bush of flowers and placed it next to where he planned to dig. Driving his shovel into the ground, pain shot through the medication and up his leg. He groaned. This was going to be a *very* long day.

He slowly made his way to the clearing. It was the perfect size and place, really. About eight feet in diameter and no trees grew in this spot. Sighing, he leaned the rake against a tree and walked to the center. He moved the bench off to the side and began digging again.

Several hours and multiple breaks later, Drew had a decent hole. He decided to quit for the day before he collapsed. While walking back to his truck to sit in the air condition, he heard leaves rustle and froze, holding his breath. He looked around, but saw nothing – no mist, no figures, nothing. Spooked, he quickly walked the rest of the way to his truck and once inside, locked the doors. He started the ignition, fully expecting a jump scare, but was surprised when nothing happened. *Maybe it was just a squirrel*, he thought.

Planning on driving back to the house, he paused while putting his truck in gear. If he were to stop now, that would mean another night in that house with her body. He wasn't sure if he could handle that, but at the same time, he wasn't sure his body could handle finishing up the hole today, either.

He decided to spend the night in a hotel. He drove back to the house and went inside to pack an overnight bag. After packing the essentials, he double checked to be sure he had enough pain medicine – some pills and a hot and cold cream. He locked the house, got back into his truck, and drove to town.

Arriving at a chain hotel, he limped up to the front desk. "Do you have any availability for tonight?" he asked.

The clerk looked him up and down. "Let me check on that for you, sir," she said. "Would you like a room on the first floor?" She noticed him limping in and her empathy kicked in.

"That would be great," he smiled.

"We've got several rooms available. How long will you be staying with us?" She glanced at him from behind her computer.

"Just tonight," he said. "You know what, make it two nights. Just in case." He handed her his card.

She ran it, half expecting it to decline, but to her surprise, the transaction was approved. She programmed the key and gave him their standard speech, pointing him in the direction of his room. He thanked her and limped off.

Once inside, he immediately tossed his bag on the bed and walked to the bathroom to turn on the shower, hoping the hot water would ease his muscles and wash away the discomfort he felt. He got in the shower and let the steaming water fall over his body. Closing his eyes, he stood there, wondering if the water would wash away his sins.

He opened his eyes and saw the swirling steam. He gasped and jumped, but then realized it was only from the water. He tried to steady his pounding heart and began thinking. Surprisingly, nothing strange had happened today. No ethereal figures, no past wives, no zombies, no screaming, no mist.

The hot water did its job and began to relax him. Maybe he was losing his mind. What other explanation could there be? Certainly there was no such thing as vengeful spirits. If so, why did she suddenly stop tormenting him last night? He shook his head, trying to clear his mind. Thoughts still racing, he grabbed the soap and began to wash up.

After staying in the shower for several more minutes, he finally emerged, feeling like a brand-new man. When was the last time he took a long, hot shower? He usually was in and out quickly, but forgot how relaxing endless hot water was.

He dressed for bed and took three more pain pills. After brushing his teeth and shutting off the lights, he fumbled for the remote and turned on the TV, not lasting five minutes before he fell asleep on the soft hotel bed.

Chapter 15

D rew awoke to a buzzing sound on the nightstand, pulling him from a comforting, dreamless sleep. He squinted at the screen, flipping through the notifications he missed, stopping on an alert from Alyssa's social media account.

He swiped the alert open, slightly anxious about what he might find. Dozens of reactions and comments littered "her" post. It felt surreal, knowing he had orchestrated that façade while carrying the weight of his secret. He closed the app and with a deep breath and tossed the phone aside, not wanting to face reality just yet.

He lay in bed, dreading the day ahead of him. He had to finish the job today. There was no question about that. His thoughts went to the dream he had the other night of her coming alive, which slowly morphed into the terrors of seeing her translucent figure in the house. It all seemed so distant as he lay in the sterile comfort of the hotel.

Knowing he couldn't let his fear rule him, he chalked up his ghostly experience to a mental break. After all, he *had* been under a lot of stress lately and his mind had felt like a jumbled mess. Trying to convince himself it was just a figment of his imagination, he decided to head back to the house.

Swinging his legs over the side of the bed, he winced at the aches, as the pain pills' effect had long since worn off. He took some more medicine and rubbed some cream on the bruised section around his ankle.

He gasped as he realized what day it was – Wednesday. Alyssa was supposed to be at work today. He quickly got dressed and headed to his truck. After speeding home, he carefully climbed the steps to the porch and unlocked the door. A strange odor filled his nostrils and he crinkled his nose. Ignoring that, he searched for her phone. He tried calling it, but it went straight to voicemail – dead. Of course it was.

If he were Alyssa, where would he put it? He tried thinking back to her last day. Was it only a couple days ago? It felt like a lifetime. After some time, and a near panic attack, Drew finally found her phone. He immediately plugged it in to charge.

His stomach growled. Looking at the clock it was no wonder he was hungry. It was nearly noon. As he let her phone charge, he threw a frozen dinner in the microwave. "No time to cook today," he sighed at his lunch choice.

Her phone buzzed, finally charged enough to power itself on. He rushed to grab it, hands slightly shaking as he entered in her password. Three missed calls and several missed texts. He quickly flipped through everything. Two calls from her boss, Charlene, and one from Jasmine.

He opened her texts next.

Two from Jasmine. "Where are you?" and "Are you alive??" Drew slightly smirked at the irony.

One from Charlene. "Alyssa. We're very worried about you. Please call me back as soon as possible." How professional.

A couple other texts from other coworkers, just generally asking if she was okay. He didn't realize how missed she would be just in the first few hours, though he should have known better.

The microwave beeped, bringing him back to reality. He needed to come up with a plan before someone showed up at the house.

He opened her boss's text thread and typed "This is Alyssa's husband, Drew. I'm sorry she didn't call earlier. She's been down with a horrible migraine. I'll have her call you as soon as she gets up." He paused and reread his message, deciding to erase that last part. He didn't want to set any expectations of her calling anyone. He pressed send, hands slightly shaking.

He contemplated responding to Jasmine, but figured the boss would relay the message down the chain. He wasn't her biggest fan. Of everyone, she was the nosiest. She seemed to give Alyssa ideas that Drew didn't agree with.

Satisfied, he put the phone down and grabbed his lunch from the microwave. After shoveling down his food, he went outside, dreading the task that lay ahead. He got into his truck and drove to the tree line.

Hours later, he was finished with the hole. He completed his task just as the sun set below the horizon and the solar lights on the trail lit up. He leaned against a tree, catching his breath. That's when he heard a sound – the rustle of leaves, this time accompanied by a faint whisper.

Fear shot through him as he looked around. He shook his head. "Get a grip," he said to himself. "Probably just a squirrel again." He felt the hairs on the back of his neck stand up as if he were being watched. Heart pounding, he spun around, looking for the culprit. He grabbed the shovel and gripped it tightly, ready for a fight.

The shadows danced around him, though the air was deathly still. In the distance, a small light flickered.

Holding his breath and imagining the cops coming, their flashlights bouncing with each step, he quickly hid behind a tree. He tried to quiet his pounding heart. Waiting a few minutes, he didn't hear any footsteps or voices so peeked his head around the tree.

Nothing.

Breathing a sigh of relief, he turned back towards the trail. The air around him suddenly felt charged, as if something were about to happen. Spinning around again, he came face to face with the spectral presence of Alyssa.

He jumped back, slightly losing his balance on his hurt leg, but quickly regained his footing. "Why are you here?" he shouted at her. "What do you want from me?"

Alyssa rolled her eyes, her personality not changing much after death. What did she want? Why was she here? She wanted revenge, obviously. She wished she could shout back at him. She wished she could do more than just appear in front of him. Patience was never her strong suit.

Willing herself with every fiber of her supernatural being, she managed to speak. "Your life," she said, voice sounding hollow.

Incredibly spooked now, Drew turned and ran as fast as he could stagger out of the woods, leaving Alyssa's ghostly form floating alone. Exceptionally proud of herself, Alyssa stood there, watching him leave, unsure of her next move. Should she follow him? Should she wait until he comes back? She slowly floated along, following him. In the distance, she saw him get into his truck and drive off. She glanced at the house and concocted a plan. A wicked smile filled her face.

That didn't just happen, Drew thought to himself as he drove towards the hotel. He realized he didn't even stop at the house to lock up. Debating whether to turn around or not, he eventually did, not wanting anyone to walk in and see Alyssa's body laying lifelessly on the bed; not that they got any visitors, especially at night.

Drew pulled into the driveway and looked around for any signs of Alyssa's ghostly form. When he saw nothing, he quickly walked to the house and began closing up. He glanced at her phone and snatched it, realizing he needed to come up with a plan about her work situation. Grabbing a fresh set of clothes from the laundry basket in the living room, he avoided the bedroom, not wanting to look at Alyssa's body. Had he taken the time to stop, he may have noticed her arm hanging at a different angle than before.

He turned off the lights as he walked out, making sure to lock to door behind him. Climbing into his truck, he started the engine and drove off in the direction of the hotel once more.

Chapter 16

Drew pulled up to the hotel and parked the truck. Clutching his fresh clothes, he headed to his room and tightly locked the door. He immediately jumped into the shower, hoping the hot water would both soothe his sore muscles and wash away the memory of what had just happened. Instead, it did the opposite.

All he could see was Alyssa's face staring at him in the swirling steam. Unable to relax, he turned off the water and got dressed. His stomach growled. Realizing he hadn't eaten much today, but unsure how he had an appetite, he grabbed his wallet and keys and headed to his truck.

He decided to go to the nearest burger joint for some cheap, greasy food. He waited to be seated and was offered the bar. Wanting to be more secluded, he asked for a booth instead. He was led to a booth in the corner and sat down.

A few minutes later, his waitress appeared. He didn't look up from his menu. She set down silverware and greeted him. "Hi, my name is Alyssa and I'll be your server tonight!" she said brightly.

His head snapped up as a wave of fear washed over him. He was met with a blond in pig tails with a little too much makeup. He breathed a sigh of relief. "Can I just get a water?" he asked weakly.

"You got it, sugar," she said as she walked off.

What are the odds, he thought to himself.

His waitress quickly returned with his water. She noticed his glazed over expression as he stared at the menu. "Need a few more minutes?" she offered in her out-of-town southern twang, trying not to startle him.

"No, no, I'm ready," he shook his head slightly to drag himself out of his thoughts. "I'll just take a well-done cheeseburger with fries."

"That comes dressed. Is that fine?" she asked.

"Yes, that'll work." He handed her back the menu.

As she walked off, he grabbed his phone. Realizing he needed to tell his wife's boss *something*, he pulled up his notes and began writing Alyssa's resignation letter. His plan was to have "Alyssa" text a very heartfelt resignation to her boss, hoping that would be the end of it. When he was just about finished, his food arrived. Thanking his waitress, he put his phone down and began eating.

Once he stuffed himself and paid, he drove back to the hotel. Opening the door, he saw his wife's ghostly figure standing there. He shook his head and closed his eyes, backing up. When he opened them again, she was gone.

"I'm really losing my mind," he muttered to himself. He sat on the bed and continued writing the resignation. Once he was satisfied, he texted it to Alyssa's phone, ready to copy it into the text thread with her boss. That's when he noticed more unread messages. He sighed and opened them.

Jasmine. "Charlene said you're sick, are you okay?"

Mom. Drew's blood ran cold. Alyssa's mother. Why did she have to reach out now? "Hey honey. Just checking in." Surely she wouldn't text back or even call if she didn't get an answer, right? They would go months without communicating. Drew decided to ignore it and deal with it later.

He went through her contacts, blocked each coworker's number, and finally texted Charlene. Once he pressed the send button he blocked her, too. Putting her phone down, he decided to try showering again, the allure of the endless hot water too much for him to resist. This time he was able to relax without incident, clearing his mind and only focusing on the running water pouring over his skin.

After what felt like hours, he emerged, skin wrinkly from the excess moisture. The cold air of the hotel room brought him back to reality. Realizing he still had work to do at the house, he glanced at the clock. 9:45. He could drive back and drag her body into the hole, but did he want to risk running into the apparition again? He didn't really have a choice. He didn't want to do it in the middle of the day, despite not having neighbors; plus, she was starting to smell.

Weighing his options, he realized he also had to get rid of the soiled mattress. Last time with Lily, he burned it and buried the coils. This time, they had a solid foam mattress. He wondered how the dense foam would burn.

Thinking it over, he decided to wait until the next day. After all, they were in the middle of several acres away from any populated area, surrounded by dense trees. Unless someone drives up the long driveway intentionally, it's likely no one even realized there was a house back there. He turned off the lights and promptly fell asleep.

The next morning, he awoke oddly early. Glancing at the clock, he groaned. *Guess it's time to get to work.* He packed up his belongings and did a sweep over the room, ensuring he didn't leave anything behind. He stopped at the counter and checked out, thanking the clerk for his stay.

The bright sunshine seemed to mock him as he drove home. Pulling up, he backed his truck to the front porch, planning on tossing Alyssa's body in the bed and driving her over to the woods. He took a deep breath and stepped out, the morning sun glaring down on him, harsh and unrelenting.

The weight of what he was about to do pressed heavily on his chest. He pushed it aside, focusing instead on the task ahead. He had a plan and plans meant control – something he desperately needed right now.

As he walked towards the house, he was lost in his thoughts. He didn't feel this much anxiety with Lily, but then again, he never saw her the way he saw Alyssa. Lily was a different breed. Timid, shy, quiet. The exact opposite of Alyssa. Lily would do as she was told and Alyssa, well, she would normally do the opposite just to spite you. Plus, Lily's ghost never haunted him, either. He sneered at the thought of shy, timid Lily trying to frighten him.

He forced his hands to stop shaking as he unlocked the front door. Opening it up, he half-expected to see her ghostly figure again. The room was still, a foul stench filling the air. He walked to the bedroom, steeling himself. He stepped past the threshold and stopped, breath hitching in his throat.

The mattress was empty except for the bindings that once held her hands to the bedframe and the blanket he had gently put over her.

She was gone.

CHAPTER 17

P anic welled up in Drew's body as he started to hyperventilate. He spun around looking for something, anything. Dashing towards the bathroom, he looked for her in there. When he glanced up in the mirror, his terrified face reflected back at him. Then he noticed something move behind him.

He spun around to see the reanimated corpse of his wife standing there, holding the same machete he threatened her with days before. "Hey baby," her raspy voice croaked out, an unnatural smile filling her face.

Drew screamed and shut the bathroom door, locking himself in.

The door shuttered as Alyssa kicked at it, yet she lacked the strength to kick it in. Drew grabbed his head, hands shaking, trying to come up with a plan. He looked around the bathroom, looking for a weapon, but found nothing. The best he had was an electric razor.

Alyssa, growing frustrated at her futile attempts to kick in the door, didn't give up. She began using the edge of the machete to try to break her way into the room. Of course, the blade was too thick, otherwise this would be a piece of cake. She decided to try to peel off the door frame, sticking the edge of the blade between the sheetrock and the wood. The wood splintered and popped up as she applied pressure on it. Grabbing the broken wood, she began tearing off pieces. When she exposed enough of the locking mechanism, she slid the blade into the now widened crack and easily opened the door.

She stepped in to find Drew in the bathtub, pressed against the wall with the electric razor in hand. "What do you plan on doing with that?" she spat. "I'm already dead, you idiot." She raised the machete and swung down on Drew's shoulder; the sound of metal slicing through flesh made a sickening squelch.

Drew screamed as he dropped the razor, his arm now hanging limply by his side. He looked at her with fear in his eyes as the wife he once knew was gone. "Alyssa! Please!" he pleaded.

What had he done? What monster did he create?

Blood pouring from his wound, he tried getting past her, but fell to his knees in the puddle of blood on the slippery tub bottom beneath his feet. She raised up the machete again, this time landing a blow on his back. He screamed again, agony shooting through his body. He looked up and grabbed her leg, trying to pull it from under her. She didn't budge.

How had she gotten so strong? Normally she wouldn't have any balance, but even using what strength he could from his single working arm didn't phase her.

She cackled and swung the machete again, cutting deep into the arm gripping her leg. He screamed again, tears pouring down his face. Is this what she felt? The terror was indescribable.

He struggled to stand, trying to escape her. Instead, she took the edge of the blade and plunged it into his chest, slightly twisting it back and forth.

Smiling, she stepped back as he fell against the wall, slowly sliding down. His blood poured down the drain. Satisfied with her work, she leaned against the vanity, watching the man she once loved struggle to breathe.

"It hurts, doesn't it baby?" she asked, still grinning. "You deserve more. You don't deserve to die just yet." He gasped as blood slowly filled his lungs.

Knowing his wounds would take some time to claim his life, she pulled the machete out and cut both of his Achilles tendons, ensuring he couldn't escape. His screams filled the air.

She sat on the floor, watching him struggle with a smile on his face. "I met Lily," she said nonchalantly. "I learned about your past." Her hand went up to gently touch the pendant still on her neck as she looked away. "She told me about this."

His eyes wide, he couldn't say anything.

"Apparently," she continued, "I wasn't the original owner of this necklace. She said you had given it to her the day you two got engaged. Which is interesting because you never told me you were married before. Of course, I never asked, which I guess is on me." She turned her attention towards him again. "She told me how in love you two were. Or so she thought. Things were going great until you started to go downhill. Sure sounds familiar, huh? She came home one day and was brutally attacked. Not like you did to me, but stabbing her 18 times, Drew? Wasn't that a little excessive? All it takes is one slit to the throat to kill someone, but no. You want to see them suffer. You want to hold that control, that power over them." She glared at him. "Do you know what my last thoughts were, Drew? How could the man I used to love do this? Now it's your time and I so wish I could make you suffer more. Unfortunately, I can't come up with the brutal plans you did, so I'm stuck with a simple stabbing." She rubbed her finger against the blade, not feeling the slice through her thumb that didn't even bleed.

"I'm...sorry," he managed to get out.

"Ha!" Alyssa spat. "Sorry? You were never sorry. You're only thinking you're sorry because this is the end. I know what you did to her after you killed her. I know what you were planning on doing to me. Why do you think I stopped you? Why do you think you fell down those stairs, Drew? That's right, that was me. Though I wasn't sure how to manifest myself yet, I realized I had the power to do *something* to you, as minor as it was. At first I was upset the fall didn't break your neck. Now looking at the pain and fear in your eyes, I'm so glad it didn't." She smiled so hard it nearly cracked her face. "I just wish Lily could see this. You'll be happy to know she moved on at last. Or at least I think she did. She finally freed herself of the weight of her past. I haven't seen her since our first meeting. I can only hope the same fate for me." Her smile turned wicked. "But if I'm stuck here, I plan on making your afterlife a living hell. You'll never rest; you'll never escape me. I'll be there, every. Single. Step. Of. The. Way!" She laughed, a cruel sound filling the air.

"Look at you," she cooed. "Drowning in your own blood. Fitting isn't it? At first you were planning on doing the same to me, weren't you? In a way, I wish you had. The agony you put me through. I don't even know how long it lasted. You played with me. You toyed with my life. You literally held it in your hands, but wouldn't give me the sweet relief of death until you had your fun. I hope you burn for eternity for what you did to me – what you did to us." She stood up. "Burn...I have an idea," she grinned and walked out of the room. "I'll be right back, baby. Don't go anywhere," she called, laughing to herself.

As she left, Drew tried to get himself out of the tub, but without working arms and his tendons severed, he was useless. He was stuck. How he wished for death. He begged for forgiveness in his mind while wishing for death before she returned. She was a monster. He couldn't imagine what she was coming back with.

A few agonizingly long minutes later, Alyssa returned with a pot of boiling water in her hands. She threw it on him, causing his skin to immediately blister as he screamed in agony again. "I know how much you like your scalding hot bathwater, baby," she giggled. Pressing the bottom of the hot pot against his face, the water and flesh sizzled as he pulled away, still screaming. "Hush now, you'll wake the neighbors," she laughed. She put the pot down on the vanity and sat down again, enjoying the sounds he was making.

"Oh, how I wish you'd talk to me, Drew," she pouted. "Then again, you never did say much, so I shouldn't be surprised. Oh well." She sat back against the wall and watched him suffer. She nodded, this was fitting for him. Not exactly what she had in mind, but fitting. Bleeding out, drowning in his own blood, and flesh burning – a precursor of what was to come, she was sure of it.

She sat in silence, watching his life slowly slip away. She crawled over to him and planted a soft kiss on his bloody lips. With his last breath, he managed to sputter out her name. "Alyssa."

Satisfied with her work, she leaned against the wall, closed her eyes, and left her body.

PART II

CHAPTER 18

It had been a couple of years since the events that changed Alyssa's existence forever. Doomed to spend her days wandering around the property alone, she was an utterly miserable soul. Drew, she could only hope and imagine, was dragged down to Hell or some form thereof. Lily moved on before Drew's...little accident.

Their bodies were found less than a week after Drew's departure, but the detectives never could figure out exactly what happened. It was clear from the condition of the bodies that Alyssa had been deceased longer than Drew, but the murder weapon – a lovely machete – only had Alyssa and Drew's fingerprints on it. There were no signs of forced entry aside from the broken pieces of wood around the bathroom lock, but no other signs of anyone else being in the home at all. It was a mystery.

Sometime later, after the mess was cleaned up and the house had been vacant for long enough, another couple bought the home. With its wraparound porch, charming red brick, and expansive acreage, it was the home of their dreams. The only thing they didn't count on was the ethereal addition that came along with it.

Evelyn Reed sat straight up in bed as a haunting scream yanked her from an otherwise peaceful slumber. A chill ran down her spine and she quickly glanced at her husband, Greyson, who didn't seem to hear the cry. She gently shook him awake.

"Honey? Greyson, did you hear that?" she whispered.

Greyson opened his eyes, glancing at her worried face. "Hear what?" He sat up, concern radiating from his body like heat waves.

"I heard a scream just now. It sounded like a woman's scream."

Greyson immediately got up to investigate. He grabbed a flashlight and began walking throughout the house then walked outside and shined around the property, looking for the source of the scream. Upon finding nothing, he headed back to the bedroom to his worried wife. "I didn't see anything. Or hear anything for that matter," he said, sitting down on the bed. "Maybe it was an animal? You know how sometimes their screams can sound human."

Evelyn pursed her lips in doubt, but eventually agreed, "Maybe you're right." She sighed and cuddled up next to her husband. She pulled him down to lay next to her and gave him a kiss on the cheek. "Thank you for checking for me."

"Of course," he said. "Now, let's go back to sleep. It's dark out, so it's definitely not time to get up."

Greyson slowly drifted to sleep, but Evelyn's mind was still on the scream she heard. Sure, it could be a fox or a bobcat, but she couldn't shake the feeling that it was something more. Visions of ghostly, shrieking women danced behind her closed eyelids.

As she lay awake, Evelyn couldn't help but let her mind run rampant. Her mind raced from phantoms to animals to demons and back, steadily thinking about the scream she heard. Finally falling asleep, her dreams were no better.

Cracking her eyes open, she realized it was daylight. She turned to her husband to find his side of the bed bare and groggily stood up, head pounding. She stopped in the bathroom to grab an over-the-counter pain pill and quickly swallowed it, hoping it would cease the throbbing. Stumbling into the kitchen, she was met with the smiling face of Greyson behind the counter.

"Good morning, sunshine. About time you got up," he teased.

Evelyn groaned and sat at the bar, putting her head against the cool countertop. "My head is killing me."

"Take anything?"

She mumbled an "mhm" and left it at that.

Greyson walked over and gently rubbed her back. "Are you hungry?" When Evelyn shook her head no Greyson sighed. "You know how grumpy you get when you miss breakfast," he teased again, hoping to make her smile. She just groaned in response. "Are you going to work today?"

This caused her to sit up. "Yes. I'm not missing for a headache."

He gave her a funny look. "You sure you want to go in?"

"Do I want to go in? No. Am I going in? Yes. As much as I'd rather stay home and go back to bed."

"Did you not sleep well or is it just the headache?" he asked skeptically.

"Well, I was awake for a while after the screaming and I don't feel like I really got a restful sleep. Maybe the headache is because of that. So, to answer your question, both I guess."

Greyson walked back to the other side of the kitchen. "Maybe some caffeine will help. Want some coffee?" He held up her favorite mug.

"Yes, please," she replied and laid her head back down on the countertop.

The scent of fresh coffee filled the air and seemed to breathe some life into Evelyn. Greyson made her coffee just how she liked it – more cream and sugar than actual coffee – and slid it over to her.

She sightly moaned as she grabbed the steaming mug and took a sip. "Thank you," she said, incredibly grateful that her husband always took care of her. Greyson moved to sit next to her with his own mug and they drank their coffee in silence. After a while she glanced up at the clock and sighed. "Guess it's time to start getting ready." She gave her husband a quick peck on the cheek and placed her empty coffee mug in the sink.

Making her way to the bedroom, she noticed that the pain in her head was subsiding, so she began her morning pre-work routine: a quick shower, get dressed, hair, makeup, shoes, and done. Her head had mostly stopped throbbing by the time she finished, much to her delight. Seems like the caffeine and medicine did their jobs.

She stepped into the living room from the bedroom and was met by the gorgeous sight of her husband, all dressed up, ready for work. She smiled and walked towards him, a grin on her face. "Maybe we should stay home today," she commented, wagging her eyebrows at him.

He laughed and rolled his eyes. "You're not the only one who doesn't want to use time off you know." He smiled and grabbed her by the waist, giving her a kiss. She threw her arms around his neck and deepened it. "But if you don't stop, I really will stay here," he murmured against her lips.

She laughed and let him go. One more quick peck and they parted ways, off to their own jobs.

CHAPTER 19

Later that night, Evelyn sat on the covered front porch, enjoying the cool breeze in the air. Dinner was in the oven – roasted chicken and veggies – so she had time to unwind, though she had an easy job – office work close to home. Greyson, however, traveled a bit farther daily for his job as a salesman, so she was always home before him. She took on the responsibility of dinner, a task she thoroughly enjoyed, often experimenting with various recipes she found online. Cleaning up after dinner was another story all together. Even with the help of their dishwasher, Evelyn still dreaded the task.

For now, though, she listened to the wind rustling the many trees on the property and the occasional buzz of carpenter bees humming through the air. As her eyes were wandering, she noticed a break in the trees. Squinting her eyes and tilting her head, she stared at the slightly overgrown, but now obvious opening.

Curious, she walked across the expansive yard, her eyes never leaving that spot. It was almost as if she were in a trance; her body continuously walking, but her mind in a daze, just staring straight ahead.

Once she arrived, she blinked and came to her senses. She first noticed flowers – lots of flowers in a row that didn't look like they belonged in the woods. As she was inspecting the plants, she noticed mini lights in the ground in between each bushy plant. "A path!" she exclaimed.

Then she felt it.

A pulling sensation in her chest. Almost as if the woods themselves were pulling her in. She glanced at her watch. Dinner only had a few minutes left and she didn't want to leave the oven unattended too long. Plus, Greyson would be home soon. She sighed and turned away, ignoring the feeling.

By the time she got inside, the timer was going off. She opened the oven door and the smell of seasonings greeted her. As she took dinner out, she heard the front door close.

"Hey, hon!" she called out. "Perfect timing; dinner is finished!"

"Sounds like you're feeling better," Greyson commented. "It smells great! Let me go change really quick. Be right back."

As Greyson walked to the bedroom, Evelyn prepped the table. She grabbed two glasses and filled both with wine. Just as Greyson came into the room, she set down the plates. They both sat.

"Another online recipe?" he asked. "It looks different this time."

"Yep! Figure it's a change from our normal chicken and veggies, so be honest on what you think; if this is a keeper or not."

As they ate, they chatted about their day. Greyson was particularly excited as he had a good feeling about a potential client he visited today. Evelyn could tell how much he loved his job. It was evident any time he spoke about it. When he was finished, Evelyn decided to tell him about the woods.

"So, guess what I saw today?"

"I can't imagine," Greyson said in-between bites with a smile on his face.

"A path!" she said excitedly. "A path in the woods! Well, it's a tad overgrown now, but there are flower bushes and lights lining it!"

Greyson raised an eyebrow. "In our woods? Where?"

"That way," she said, pointing in the general direction as if he could tell where she was pointing to while inside the house.

"Well, let's go check it out," he said, finishing his last piece of broccoli. She squealed in excitement and picked up their plates.

Luckily it was still light outside. She led him to the spot in the woods, half expecting it to be her imagination, but no, there it was in all its overgrown glory.

"Hmm," Greyson stroked his beard in thought. "Wanna go on an adventure?"

"Really?" Her eyes beamed up at him.

"Really. I'm as curious as you are," he said as he took a step into the overgrowth. She fell in line behind him, careful not to step on any lights or plants. They walked for a few minutes, following the half-hidden lights in the ground. Suddenly, he stopped. "Look at this."

She stepped beside him and took in their surroundings. A circle shaped clearing with a bench off to the side and directly in the middle – a huge hole with a mound of dirt next to it.

"What...what is this?" Evelyn asked, suddenly wary.

Greyson slowly stepped towards the hole. Glancing down he suddenly felt terribly uncomfortable. "I think we should go," he said, turning towards his wife.

"Is there anything in it?" She peered around him, curious.

"No, but I don't think it was meant for a flower bed," he stated glancing back at the hole. "Let's go. We need to do some research."

"Are you thinking..." she trailed off.

"Yeah," he said. He grabbed her hand. "I really think we should go."

She let him lead her back down the path towards the house, occasionally stealing a glance behind them. When they arrived, he grabbed his phone and sat on the couch. He began his search with the address. When nothing but real estate websites popped up, he took a different route. He typed in *New Woogrea, MN murder*.

"Anything?" Evelyn asked as she sat down next to him.

He shook his head, waiting for the page to load. There it was. He clicked the first link that popped up - a news website - and quickly scanned the article. His face paled.

Evelyn, studying him closely, saw the change in his demeanor, but kept quiet until he finished. Shocked into silence, he wordlessly handed her the phone. She read the headline. *Couple Found in New Woogrea Home*. She checked the date – about two years ago. Her brow furrowed as she slowly read the article. After she finished, she handed him the phone and grabbed hers.

She searched for the names mentioned in the article: *Alyssa and Drew Stanton*. She found their obituaries, social media pages, but nothing really useful. She then searched their names and the address of the house.

Her blood ran cold.

"Greyson..." Her hands started to shake. "Look." He turned his attention from his phone to hers. He squinted his eyes and then widened them as he realized what he was reading. "They lived here!" she cried. "They were killed in this house!"

"We don't know that for sure," he began.

"Did you read the same article I did? Alyssa and Drew Stanton. A search with this address brings up the public records with them *at this address* – their last known address at that. Oh, Greyson, why didn't anyone tell us?"

"I don't know. Shouldn't that have been disclosed to us before we bought this place?" He opened his phone again to search the laws. "Great," he said after a minute. "In Minnesota, it doesn't have to be disclosed."

"So that hole we saw…"

"We don't know that," Greyson said again, more gently this time.

"What else could it be? It's the perfect size. Oh no, no, no. I don't know if I can stay here knowing that. What if the killer comes back? What if they haunt us? What-"

"Baby, baby, shh." He tried calming her down, placing a hand on her shoulder. "How long have we been here? Nothing's happened. No killers, no ghosts, no mysterious circumstances. I think we're okay."

"I've got to know how they died. The article wasn't really informative on that part."

"I don't know if that's a good idea. You're already freaked out enough."

"It might help? I don't know. Maybe I just need to know." She bit her lip, her mind racing with possibilities. "Screw it, I'm going to do it." She grabbed her phone and began her research. After scanning through several articles, she finally found what she was looking for. "Greyson, I think I found it. Listen to this: Alyssa's body was found with bruising around her face and neck, indicating she had been asphyxiated also with evidence of sexual abuse. Drew was found with multiple wounds and severe burns on his body. A machete and an empty pot were found in the room the bodies were found in, leading investigators to believe Drew was burned with boiling water and tortured. There were no signs of forced entry. This is an ongoing investigation."

"That's…that's horrible. I didn't know they wrote details like that in news articles," Greyson said, shocked.

"This is brutal. How did we not hear about this?" Evelyn looked up from her phone, concern in her eyes.

"I don't know. Are the articles you're reading local or national news outlets?"

"Mostly local, but wouldn't you think that something this cruel would make the national news? Especially if they haven't found the guy?"

"Maybe there's more to the story and they're keeping it hush-hush so there aren't any copycats. You know how sick people are." He frowned, a disgusted look on his face.

"You're right. I'm going to see if there's a more recent article saying this guy has been caught."

"Just don't go too deep into the rabbit hole. You'll probably have nightmares," Greyson warned.

"I'll be fine," she said as she waved a hand in his direction, dismissing his concerns.

Chapter 20

Later that night, Evelyn lay awake in bed again. She had found an online forum with more information on the case, though she slightly questioned its validity. According to the people on there, there was no evidence of anyone else in the house and only the husband and wife's fingerprints showed up on the search. Also, only the husband's DNA had been found on her and his fingerprints were all over her neck. But how? Surely it couldn't be murder-suicide with those wounds inflected on both. Evelyn had also found the crime scene photos and immediately regretted it.

The woman in the pictures looked almost peaceful in a decaying sort of way. Her greenish blackish body lay against the wall, head tilted backwards as if she were resting. Her once fair skin was slipping and was dotted with small fluid-filled blisters. Dried unknown fluid surrounded her mouth and her abdomen was distended.

Drew, on the other hand, looked like he had died in agony. His blackening body was mangled and crammed in the small space of the bathtub. Dried blood was crusted around his lips and on his clothing, caked beneath his body, and splattered on the walls. His discolored face and neck were covered in large angry blisters. He lay slumped forward over the edge, with one arm seemingly reaching for Alyssa, his completely black fingertips hanging just out of reach from her.

The pictures depicted every angle of the couple, showcasing every gruesome detail.

Her mind raced. It made no sense. Who killed Alyssa and Drew Stanton? Is it the same person that dug the hole? Why would they bury a body on the same property the couple was killed on? Why in such an obvious place with the path, the bench, and the clearing? Evelyn had so many questions.

After tossing and turning, she finally fell asleep. Just as Greyson predicted, she had nightmares. She found herself running into the woods, down the same path she and Greyson had explored earlier that day. She wasn't sure what she was running from, but felt chased. Her heart pounded in her ears as she made her way to the clearing. She stopped and spun around, looking for her would be assailant. Not seeing anything, she felt her panic slightly subside.

Then she heard a voice. She tried to listen over the pounding of her beating heart, but the voice was quiet. She couldn't make out the words, but it sounded feminine. It seemed as if it were coming from the large hole in the ground. Evelyn looked around again and didn't see anything, so she slowly walked closer to the hole. The voice stopped as she peered inside, seeing nothing. Hearing leaves crunch, she spun her head around. "Greyson," she breathed, a sigh of relief escaping her lips.

Greyson said nothing, eyes staring blankly ahead as he walked towards his wife.

"What's wrong?" she asked, taking a step forward. Something glinted in the light. She looked down to see a shining machete in his hand. "Greyson...what..." Instinctively she backed up. "Greyson!"

Ever silent, he continued walking towards her. His hand gripped tighter on the machete.

"Please, stop this!" she begged. She took another step backwards, her foot slipping on the edge of the hole. She screamed as she fell, landing with an "Oof." She clenched her jaws and sucked in air between her teeth, looking down at her arm, which she was sure she had broken. She saw Greyson peer over the edge of the hole, staring down at her with the same blank eyes. "Greyson, please..." she pleaded again.

He turned his back to her and walked away.

"Greyson!" she shouted. Biting her lip, she stood up and looked around. There was nothing. No roots to grab ahold of; no mysterious ladder appearing out of thin air; nothing to save her. She was stuck.

She turned around and came face to face with the spectral figure of a woman with a shining pendant at her throat. Evelyn screamed and backed up as much as the small hole would allow. The figure didn't move.

Evelyn began hyperventilating. She was stuck. Her arm was broken. There was a transparent woman standing in front of her. Tears began to well up in her eyes as she tried to catch her breath through the gasps.

Suddenly, the figure let out a horrifying shriek and quickly flew towards Evelyn. She shut her eyes and abruptly bolted straight up in bed, still breathing heavily, drenched in sweat, but otherwise fine. She glanced at her husband, lying peacefully next to her, blissfully unaware of Evelyn's panic.

Petrified, but not wanting to wake Greyson, she scooted over towards him and pressed her back against his body. Instantly feeling some comfort, she replayed the nightmare in her head. She had a feeling she wasn't going to get much more sleep tonight.

The night dragged on as Evelyn lay pressed against her sleeping husband. While she was terrified to fall back asleep, she knew she needed the rest. She made a silent vow to never step foot in those woods again.

When the alarm finally went off, she groggily dragged herself out of bed. She turned and gently pushed on Greyson's shoulder. "Hey hon, it's time to get up." He stretched and groaned, clearly not ready for the morning.

"Morning," he said, voice thick with sleep. He glanced over to her and sat up. "You look awful. What's wrong?"

"Oh, gee, thanks," she said flatly.

"I didn't mean it like that and you know it."

"I couldn't sleep. Nightmares."

"I hate to be the one to say I told you so. Wanna talk about them?"

"No, not really," she turned to go to the kitchen.

He stared after her. It was unusual she didn't want to talk about what was bothering her. She was hiding something, he felt it. Or maybe it was just her lack of sleep.

After a few minutes, Greyson joined Evelyn in the kitchen. She had already made him a cup of coffee and had it sitting on the bar. "Breakfast?" she asked.

"Not feeling anything extravagant. Frozen waffles?" he suggested.

"Sure," she replied quietly.

"Really, please tell me what's wrong. This isn't like you." She took out the butter and syrup from the fridge, sighed, and dove into telling him about the dream. After she was finished, he was quiet. "You know I'd never hurt you, right?"

"I know. I'm not in the least bit worried about that. It just shook me up is all. I guess I shouldn't read scary stuff before bed." She softly chuckled as she took the waffles out of the toaster.

He slightly smirked and gratefully took his waffle. "You know," he said, his mouth full. "Maybe we should fix up that path." Evelyn paled.

He noticed her expression and quickly explained himself. "What I mean is, maybe if we restore it to its former glory and fill in that hole, it'll be like closing a door for you."

"What would be closing a door is letting that thing overgrow and never setting foot in there again," she said flatly.

Greyson raised his hands in surrender. "Okay, okay. Whatever makes you more comfortable."

She stayed silent. Not reading those articles and looking at the pictures would have made her more comfortable. Too late for that though.

Finishing their breakfast in silence, Greyson looked at the clock. "Guess it's time to get ready."

"I really don't feel like going in today. I'm exhausted."

"Do you think it's a good idea to stay here by yourself though? I mean, whatever you want to do, but I don't want you calling in and regretting it."

"You're right. Ugh. Guess I'll go hop in the shower." She got up and headed towards the bedroom.

She felt slightly more human after showering and dressing, though she was far from looking forward to work. Her overly observant coworkers are going to notice something's up. She had never been a great liar, but maybe she can chalk it up to just not sleeping well, which was mostly the truth.

She gave Greyson a quick kiss and they went about their day.

Chapter 21

When she arrived at work, Evelyn debated staying in her car until the very last minute, just to avoid people. She sighed and abandoned that idea, steeling herself for the barrage of questions that were sure to come.

While she's normally grateful for such supportive coworkers, today she just wasn't feeling it. Then an idea hit her. Maybe she can get information on the couple from them. Most of these people have lived in the area their whole lives. Nearly forgetting her dream, her morbid curiosity kicked in and she walked towards the office.

Why do you want to torture yourself, Evelyn? she thought to herself. *Didn't you already have enough nightmares about this?*

"Well, look what the cat dragged in," a feminine voice interrupted her thoughts.

"What?" Evelyn looked down at her watch then back up at her coworker. "I'm 20 minutes early!"

"Yeah, but you look like hell."

Evelyn scoffed, wondering why she bothered with the makeup if this was going to be how she was greeted. "Just didn't sleep well."

"Ohhh," her coworker waggled her eyebrows. "So that's what we're calling it now?"

"Jasmine!" Evelyn flushed. "It's not like that. At least not this time." She winked.

"Sure, sure," Jasmine said as she followed Evelyn to her office.

"Okay, serious talk. I have a question for you," she said as she set down her briefcase and purse. "Have you ever heard of Alyssa and Dean Stanton?"

Jasmine froze. "Yes," she answered carefully.

"What do you know about them?"

"Why are you asking?" Jasmine tried not to sound defensive.

"Well," Evelyn began. "Greyson and I were exploring the property and found a path in the woods leading to a clearing. In the clearing was a bench...and a huge hole."

"Uh huh," Jasmine encouraged, not yet connecting the dots.

"Well," Evelyn said again. "Greyson had a bad feeling about the hole so we started digging online. Turns out this couple, Alyssa and Dean Stanton, were murdered in our house!"

Jasmine's jaw dropped. "Wait, wait. You're telling me you bought *their* house? And that's where you've been living?"

"Yes..." Evelyn replied skeptically. "Why? What do you know?"

Jasmine looked at her watch. "We only have a few minutes, so we'll have to continue this later, but Alyssa used to work here." Evelyn's jaw dropped as she pulled up Alyssa's social media page, pausing slightly at the sight of her friend's smiling face. Tears welled up in her eyes, threatening to spill over. She shook her head and cleared her throat, then showed Evelyn the progress pictures of the path. "This what you found?"

"Yes!" Evelyn exclaimed. "That's it!"

Letting out a breath, Jasmine hesitated. "We'll catch up on this during lunch. I've got a meeting shortly and I can't be late." She turned and waved at Evelyn and walked back to her office.

Every few minutes Evelyn was checking the clock. It was almost as if it were frozen. Time just seemed to drag on today. She and Alyssa lived in the same house; worked in the same office. If Alyssa had a career in insurance, then it wasn't surprising she worked at the only agency in this town – after all, it was much better than commuting to the city to work at one.

She thought back to how she got this job and if the two were related, but decided that too much time had passed between Alyssa's death and Evelyn moving into town and it must have just been a coincidence; an eerie coincidence.

When noon hit, she jumped up, grabbed her sandwich, and quickly walked to Jasmine's office. "Do you have lunch?"

"Yep!" Jasmine pulled a glass dish of leftovers from the mini fridge in the corner. "Let me go heat this up and I'll be right back."

Jasmine returned a couple minutes later and sat down. "Okay. So. We know you live in Alyssa's old house. We know she and Drew were found...dead," she hesitated at the last word. "What we – or nobody – knows is how."

"What can you tell me about Alyssa?" Evelyn asked between bites.

Jasmine smiled softly, thinking of the good times and the laughs she and Alyssa shared then hesitated again. "She was strong spirited. She and Drew had problems and a lot of them. It seems they were constantly fighting about something. Even though he had a job, I always thought he was a good-for-nothing." She made a sour face. "She seemed to be happy at times, but he didn't seem to treat her right. Nothing major like beating her or anything, but just subtle things, you know?" She stopped and shut her eyes and took a deep breath. "Shortly before she...disappeared...Alyssa told me about this pull she felt. She felt as though the woods were calling her. I thought it was extremely strange. I mean, who has those types of feelings? Looking back on it now," she paused and looked upwards at nothing in particular as a tear slipped down her cheek, "maybe it was her gut telling her something was coming."

Nearly finished her sandwich now, Evelyn asked, "Do *you* have any thoughts on who could have done it? I read some pretty brutal things online about it last night."

"If you ask me, I think Drew did it," Jasmine replied with a bitter expression.

Evelyn gasped. "What?! How?"

"I don't know since he turned up dead, too. But they were in the middle of another fight and she mentioned to me that she told him she was thinking of leaving him. I wonder if he snapped." To Evelyn, it seemed easier for her to talk about Drew than Alyssa.

"Do you think he had that in him?" Evelyn asked incredulously.

Jasmine took another bite. "I only met him a handful of times throughout the years of her working here, but from the way she described him when they were fighting, I'd say it's possible."

Silently thinking, Evelyn fiddled with her fingers. "So, if he killed her, which would sorta make sense since his fingerprints were on her neck-" Jasmine flinched and shut her eyes. "Sorry! But if he did it, who got him? Surely she didn't come back to life to exact revenge."

"She was talking about the possibility of being a werewolf," Jasmine mused, eyes getting misty again. After seeing Evelyn's skeptical look, she clarified. "She was kidding. But if anyone would come back from the grave for revenge, it would be Alyssa."

Evelyn pondered. She hadn't really gotten any further than she was before. "What do other people think? I know people talk."

Rolling her eyes, Jasmine scoffed. "Who cares what other people say? It's all speculation anyway. The cops haven't found anything and all people can do is talk."

Realizing she pushed far enough, Evelyn quickly apologized and changed the subject. They finished out their lunch break chatting about their weekend plans. Evelyn couldn't wait to get home to update Greyson on what she found out.

As Evelyn pulled into the driveway, she noticed Greyson's car already there. "That's odd," she murmured, checking the clock to be sure she wasn't late. She parked and walked to the door. "Hey there," she called out.

"In the living room!" he shouted.

She walked to the living room and found Greyson on the couch, watching some infomercial. Hearing her approach, he turned his attention to her. He stood up and gave her a quick kiss. "How was work?"

"You won't believe what I found out today," she said as she sat on the couch. "Not only did Drew and Alyssa Stanton live *in this house*, but Alyssa actually worked *at my job*!"

Greyson sat up straight. "What?! How did you find out?!"

"I was talking to Jasmine about the situation, hoping to get some more information. Turns out they were pretty close and they knew each other on a personal level. And get this – Jasmine thinks Drew did it!"

"How? He was found dead, too."

She shrugged. "Dunno, but that's her theory. I just think it's crazy – this house, that hole, now my job? What, did Drew work at your place, too?"

"I can ask," Greyson said hesitantly.

"No, I'm being facetious," she waved a hand in the air, dismissing his offer. "I don't think I'd want to know if he did. I'd have to move out."

"Why? Just because some people died in this house and in this Podunk, you just happened to work in the same office as one of the victims? There aren't that many insurance agencies here."

"When you say it like that, it sounds so logical," Evelyn said sarcastically. "Did you just hear yourself?"

Greyson gently put his hand on her shoulder. "You're working yourself up over this. Is it creepy? Yes. Is it worth losing our dream house over? No." Evelyn pursed her lips, but didn't say anything. He sighed. "Look, I'm not dismissing you. I totally understand where you're coming from. I just don't want you working yourself up and freaking out over something that we can't change and that really has no bearing on our lives."

She lifted her head and looked into his eyes. "I guess you're right."

He brushed a strand of hair from her face. "I mean it, I'm not dismissing you at all. You already had a rough night over this. I don't want you to stress any more over it."

She gently grabbed his hand and held it. "I get it. I'm not upset with you, I promise." She turned his hand and kissed it. "On that note, I'm super tired. Come to bed with me soon?" His eyes sparkled as he waggled his eyebrows. "No," she immediately said as she got up to walk towards the kitchen. He chuckled in response.

"I'm making some toast for dinner before bed. Want some?" she called from the kitchen.

"Wait, you're really going to bed after dinner?" he asked incredulously. "It's barely six o'clock."

"Some of us didn't get enough rest last night, Sleeping Beauty."

That caused him to chuckle again. "Alright, alright. It's a bit too early for me, but I'll tuck you in after you eat."

"Oh! I was so enamored by what Jasmine told me that I didn't even ask how your day was or why you were home early." Evelyn felt terrible that she dominated the conversation without even asking about his day first.

"Remember the potential client I had been working with? He agreed to sign the contract today! That's a *1.2-million-dollar contract*!" He beamed, obviously extremely proud of himself.

"That's amazing! Congratulations! This calls for a celebration!" She grabbed two wine glasses and the good wine from the cabinet. "Why didn't you say something earlier?"

"I figured I'd get to it eventually. You seemed about ready to burst with your news."

"Well, yeah, but your news is bigger! I hope your boss sees it and rewards you with a nice bonus. You've been working on this client for months."

"I'm not holding my breath," Greyson said, rolling his eyes. "You know how he is. But whatever, where's that wine?"

She handed him a glass and lifted hers in the air in a toast. "To big contracts and new beginnings." They clinked glasses and each took a sip. They aimlessly chatted as they finished their wine. When they finished, Evelyn moved to put the glasses in the dishwasher.

"Go to bed. I've got this," Greyson walked over and grabbed the glasses from her hands.

"It's just putting two glasses into the dishwasher. I've got this," she stuck out her tongue at him, but smiled at his thoughtfulness as she moved to the couch.

"Thought you were going to bed?" he asked, raising an eyebrow.

"It's barely seven. If I go to bed now I'll wake up at the butt-crack of dawn. Definitely not how I want to spend my Saturday morning."

He sat down next to her and grabbed the TV remote. "Good point. In the mood for anything in particular tonight?" He gestured towards the TV with the remote.

"Mmm," she looked up at the ceiling as she thought. "What about a cooking show? You know how much I love watching amateur chefs getting screamed at." She moved to snuggle against him and lay her head on his shoulder.

"Psychopath," he laughed as he began flipping through the menu to find an episode. He noticed after about 30 minutes that she had fallen asleep on him. He smiled and decided not to move and let her rest. He stared at the TV in a daze, not paying attention to what was playing, instead thinking about what they found out about the previous residents. He didn't want to cause her to be frightened any more than she was already, but he had some concerns about the situation as well.

He wasn't terribly superstitious, but had to admit he had had a bad feeling since they found the hole. If they hadn't found out about the deaths, he could chalk it up to his imagination, but now that they had...

Evelyn stirred and he looked down at her. She opened her eyes and glanced up at him. Instead of the sleepy smile he expected, her eyes looked blank, like she wasn't really there. "Evelyn?" he asked softly. "Are you ready to go to bed? This can't be comfortable for you."

Something about her expression changed, but he couldn't put his finger on it. The corners of her mouth twitched and her eyes regained some focus, but were off somehow. Suddenly she moved off him and glared.

"What's wrong?" he asked, concerned now.

She stayed silent, but continued to give him the glaring look. She blinked hard and the expression was gone. No longer glaring, she looked up at him sleepily. "What's the matter?" she asked, yawning.

"Did you have a bad dream about me or something?" Greyson asked, confused.

"No," she yawned again and stretched. "Was I supposed to?"

"You woke up and glared at me like I was the most vile human being on the planet. It lasted a few seconds then you were, well, you again."

Evelyn scrunched up her nose and squinted her eyes, clearly confused by what he was telling her. "I did? I don't remember that."

"Maybe it was the beginning stages of sleepwalking," he shrugged.

"But I've never done that before," she argued.

He brushed it off as her not getting enough sleep. "It's fine, don't worry about it. Now, are you ready for bed or do you want to try to stay up and actually watch a full episode?" He loved teasing her and took every opportunity he had to throw a little playful jab in just to gently push her buttons. He especially enjoyed it when she teased back. A little playful banter kept their relationship light and prevented things from getting too serious or too boring.

"I think I'm just going to go to bed and hope I don't wake up too early. That way you can watch something you want and do what you need to do to unwind." She stood up, back cracking from the awkward position she had been in for the past half-hour.

He smirked at her. "I can think of something to help me unwind. We do need to celebrate." He gave her a wink.

"Perv," she said as she rolled her eyes at him and walked with him to the bedroom. "Rain check? Definitely not up for anything tonight."

"I know. But I will take that rain check. Expect me to cash it in soon." He gave her a goofy grin. She just sighed in response, clearly not awake enough to pick back.

She fell asleep seconds after her head hit the pillow.

Chapter 22

Evelyn opened her eyes to darkness. Greyson wasn't in bed, so she figured she hadn't been asleep that long. She turned around and saw something glinting. Trying to focus, she couldn't make it out. Reaching over on the nightstand, she clicked on the lamp and gasped.

Standing at the end of her bed was a woman. She was wearing a short dress with a low-cut neckline. Her brown hair was loose around her shoulders and she wore a shining silver and red pendant around her throat.

Bolting upright and shocked speechless, Evelyn couldn't get words out. A hundred questions ran through her mind at once. *Are we being robbed? Is Greyson okay? What does she want? How did she get in here? Is she the killer and we're next?*

Evelyn finally found her voice. "Who are you?" she whispered. The woman stood silent. "What do you want? Where's Greyson?" she asked, louder this time. Silence. "Get out of our house!"

Suddenly the bedroom door opened. Evelyn snapped her head towards the sound, expecting the worst, but saw it was only Greyson. She quickly turned her head back to the end of the bed, but the woman was gone. Had she imagined it?

"I thought I heard your voice. Talking to yourself again or was this another not-sleepwalking episode?" he asked.

"Did you see her?" Evelyn turned towards her husband, face pale.

"See who?" Greyson looked around, seeing nothing out of place.

"There was a woman. A woman at the end of the bed. She was wearing a dress and had brown hair. Oh and a necklace – that's what caught my attention I guess..." she trailed off, realizing how insane she sounded.

Greyson walked to the edge of the bed and sat down, his face full of concern. "What are you talking about?"

"I'm saying there was someone in here! I think it was Alyssa!" she exclaimed, frustrated he wasn't understanding.

"Alyssa? Sweetheart, there was no one here. No one came in or out of this room or the house for that matter. It's just you and me here." He put his hand over hers, trying to sooth her. "Maybe you were still asleep?"

"Oh, so now I'm seeing things?" she accused.

"I didn't say that. I said maybe you were asleep still. There's a difference. It could have been a dream."

"No, she was there. I felt her eyes on me in the darkness. I saw her clear as day!"

"Okay, okay," he raised his hands in surrender. "What do you want me to do?"

"Can you please go check everything out?" she pleaded. "Then come to bed with me? I don't really want to be alone right now."

She was more shaken up than he thought. "Of course I'll go check. Give me a few minutes and I'll be right back," he said as he walked out the bedroom.

Waiting for Greyson to return seemed to be the longest couple of minutes of Evelyn's life. She nervously looked around, got out of bed, checked the bathroom, checked the closet, looked under the bed, paced, and finally got back into bed. She was sitting straight up when he walked back into the room.

He shook his head. "There's nothing out of place. It doesn't look like anyone was here."

"Where could she have gone? I swear, Greyson. I swear I saw her here. She was clear as day!"

"Shh, it's okay." He got into bed and wrapped his arms around her, softly laying her down, but not releasing his gentle grip. He pulled her close and stroked her hair. "I've got you. Everything's okay, I promise." Her body felt incredibly tense in his arms and she was trembling slightly. Wanting to relax her, he turned her and said, "Lay on your stomach. I'm going to rub your back." She obliged, but her movements were stiff.

He grabbed the lotion, lifted her shirt slightly, and began rubbing her in silence. After a while he felt her muscles finally relax. He stopped and listened to her breathing – it was even and steady. She must be asleep. "Babe?" he whispered. No answer. He softly smiled and stretched to turn off the lamp.

It was his turn to lay awake, too rattled for sleep. He let his mind wander. He thought about the new client, the couple and their deaths, and now the woman in their bedroom. It's not like Evelyn to see things. She's never been one to get spooked easily. There had to be an explanation for what she saw. He wasn't convinced she was fully awake, just the same as her episode earlier. He was grateful when he felt sleep finally creep up on him, finally drifting into a dreamless slumber.

The rising sun shone through the sheer curtains of the bedroom, its bright rays slowly illuminating the room. Once the rays reached Evelyn's eyes, she woke up and groaned. "It's too early for this." She threw the comforter over her head and tried to go back to sleep. The previous night's events hit her like a jolt and her eyes snapped open. Remembering the details of the woman's appearance, her heart started pounding harder as the vision of the woman's empty eyes appeared in her head. She instinctively pressed her back against Greyson.

She couldn't explain the unease she felt. The woman did nothing but stand there; granted, she didn't belong in their house, but she didn't try to harm Evelyn. She didn't try to do anything at all. She just stood there. Evelyn tried to steady her breathing and relax, the woman's face never leaving her mind. She couldn't shake the feeling that she was Alyssa.

Beside her, Greyson stirred. He turned and wrapped his arms around her, pulling her close. She smiled, snuggling into his embrace. "Morning," she whispered. He groaned in response. She folded her arms around his, holding onto him. Knowing he wasn't ready to get out of bed, she quietly lay there, safe in his arms. After a while she figured he was asleep again or never really woke up. Feeling lazy, she snuggled deeper into him and tried going back to sleep herself.

Her mind was way too active already to fall back asleep. She ran through the possibilities of who the unknown woman could be, if not Alyssa. She was no closer to unraveling the mystery when Greyson finally awoke. She felt his body move as he released her and stretched. "Morning beautiful," he kissed her head.

"About time you woke up," she gently elbowed his stomach. "I've been up forever."

"Not my fault you can't sleep," he yawned and wrapped her in his arms again.

"Going back to sleep already?" she teased.

"Nah, just cuddling. Why? Are you in a hurry to go somewhere?" he lightly pressed his face against her neck.

"It's Saturday. I have nowhere to be and nowhere I'd rather be than here."

"Great answer." He swiftly grabbed her and pulled her under him, holding himself above her, and looked down into her eyes. She just raised an eyebrow in response. He smirked and leaned down to kiss her. She reciprocated and deepened the kiss, putting her arms around his neck, pulling him to her.

His hands softly trailed along her body, pushing up her shirt to feel her skin. She moved her arms from around him to take off his shirt and pulled him to her again, kissing him. They broke free long enough to quickly strip and then pressed against each other again.

He moved his lips from her mouth, along her jawline, down to her neck. She quietly gasped and moaned, goosebumps forming on her skin. Gently trailing her fingernails down his back, she felt his body shudder against hers. He trailed kisses down her collarbone, leading to her breasts. He lightly breathed on one of her nipples and it instantly hardened. He smirked and took it in his mouth, tongue swirling around. She moaned again and arched her back, pressing her breast into him.

"Can't forget you," he said as he moved to the other one. She bit her lip, her desire building.

"Please..." she whispered. He ignored her and trailed kisses down her stomach and down her thighs. Her breath hitched as he hovered over her most sensitive area. "Please," she whispered again, louder this time.

He trailed his fingers along her body, enjoying the feel of her skin. Then he bent his head and began slowly exploring her with his tongue. She gasped at his touch. He continued to tease her, loving hearing his name on her lips. She began to breathe heavily and he could hardly contain his desire for her. He moved up and kissed her neck. "Ready?" he breathed. She only whimpered in response.

He slowly and gently entered her, causing another moan to erupt from her. He tenderly moved his body, gradually picking up pace. She grabbed his hips and somehow pulled him even closer to her. Releasing his hips and running her fingernails down his back again, she reached up and grabbed his mouth with hers, biting his lip, knowing how to push all of his buttons. Recognizing her cue, he picked up the pace.

He moaned as he thrusted inside of her. She bit her lip to keep quiet, wanting to enjoy the sounds he made. "Don't hide those beautiful moans from me," he breathed. She released her lip. Her breathing quickened as she struggled to keep the rhythm, the pleasure threatening to override her body. Feeling her tighten around him pushed Greyson over the edge. He thrust once more and loudly moaned, finishing inside her. She screamed his name and arched her back, feeling her pleasure explode.

They lay there entangled in each other's embrace, sweaty and breathing heavily. "What a way to start the morning," Evelyn breathed. Greyson just chuckled in response. "Guess that was you cashing in that rain check?"

"Oh, was it? I thought that was just for fun," he gave her a wink.

"Well, I have to admit, it *was* fun," she grinned and snuggled more into him. "So, what's on the agenda for today?"

"Can't we just have a lazy day? Lounge around the house. Maybe have some more fun?"

Laughing, she replied, "That's always on your mind you perv. We do need to do some chores. Laundry isn't going to wash itself, floors need to be swept and mopped, bathrooms-"

"Okay, okay I get it," he grumbled.

"We could save all that for Sunday," she suggested, mind elsewhere.

He sighed. "No, let's get it all done today. That way it's out of the way."

"Fine by me," she replied. They lay in silence for a while longer, enjoying each other's company. After a while, Evelyn spoke up. "So, umm, I think I want to go back into the woods."

Greyson sat up and looked at her like she had lost her mind. "Are you serious? After your nightmares you really think it's a good idea?"

She shrank back a little bit and shrugged. "I don't know. Maybe it'll help ease my mind. Maybe it'll make things worse. I won't know until I go back there. Something about this whole situation has me fascinated, yet terrified at the same time. I can't get it off my mind."

"You don't say. I hadn't noticed," he said semi-sarcastically. "I don't know if this is a good idea, but if it's something you want to do, I won't stop you, you know that. Aside from some sort of closure, what are you trying to accomplish?"

"I guess you said it yourself – some sort of closure. I'm not exactly a fan of nightmares and seeing things like strange women and if coming to terms with what's in there will help, then I need to do it." She sat up and steeled herself. "Yes. I think I have to do this."

Greyson sighed. "If you think that'll help, then I'm on board. Let's go in there today."

Evelyn bit her lip. "So soon?"

He rolled his eyes. "Didn't you just say you wanted to go back? Why push it off and risk you stressing yourself out over the thought of it, having more nightmares, and seeing other things? I think if you believe it'll help, then we need to do this sooner rather than later."

"I guess you're right. Let's shower and dress. Oh, and breakfast because ya girl is hungry," she said, trying to lighten the mood.

An hour later they were walking outside towards the clearing across the yard. Evelyn's heart raced and though Greyson didn't let it show, his heart was, too. The sun was high up in the sky, its light filtering through the canopy of trees, casting light shadows throughout the woods. They carefully stepped through the brush, following the overgrown path lined by brightly colored flowers.

About halfway to the bench, and subsequently the hole, Evelyn heard barely audible whispers. Initially thinking it was Greyson talking to himself, she ignored them, but the deeper they went into the woods, the louder the whispers became. Goosebumps formed on her arms, despite the warm temperature. Not wanting to alarm her husband, she tried convincing herself it was the whisper of the wind through the trees. After what felt like eternity they arrived at the clearing. The whispers were louder here. Unable to discern what was being said, Evelyn tried her best to ignore them and focus on what was in front of her.

She jumped when Greyson spoke. "Okay, we're here. Now what?"

"Umm," she hesitated. "I'm not sure. I didn't think this far ahead."

Sighing, he sat on the bench. "Do you feel any better? More relaxed at all?"

She contemplated telling him about the whispers she was hearing. "Well," she began, but decided against it and steered away from the topic. "No, not really." She walked over to the hole and peered inside. It wasn't nearly as deep as in her dream. Relief washed over her, though she wasn't sure why. Maybe this wasn't what they were thinking it was. After all, why would a killer dig a grave on the property and just abandon it – one of the same questions they had when they first discovered the hole. "Maybe it was for a dog and this was going to be a memorial site," she offered.

Greyson thought about her suggestion for a little bit, not wanting to think of the other possibilities this hole had been dug for. "That's actually a good thought. It's not terribly large and we really don't know much about the history of this place. What do you say about us putting the dirt back and making this a little get-away area?"

She considered his proposal. Filling in the hole and clearing this area would probably change the atmosphere from overgrown and eerie to open and inviting. The flowers were a nice touch and the bench was in the perfect location. "Okay," she agreed. "Let's do it!" The whispers subsided. She hoped this change would squash her apprehension about this place.

CHAPTER 23

Later that night after showers and dinner, Evelyn and Greyson heavily plopped down on the couch. "We did good," she commented.

"We? I did most of the work," he teased.

She scoffed, "I helped!"

"Barely." He grinned at her, playfully elbowing her side. She rolled her eyes in response.

Evelyn never did mention the whispers, but didn't hear them again once they started filling in the hole. *It must have been the trees,* she thought. She stared at the TV, not really paying attention to what was playing, unable to shake the slight unease lingering from earlier. Grabbing her phone, she decided to do some more research. Remembering Jasmine showing her Alyssa's social media page and the posts about the path, she was determined to find out whether Alyssa and her husband had a dog.

Searching through several Alyssa Stanton profiles, she suddenly gasped. Greyson turned his head to look at her inquisitively. "Greyson!" she exclaimed. "That *was* her!"

He looked over at her phone, seeing Alyssa's name and profile picture. "Yes?" he asked tentatively. "Her face matches the media pictures of her. So, what of it?"

"No, you don't understand! That *is* who I saw last night! Look, she's wearing the same pendant!"

Greyson looked closer, skeptical of her claims. He noticed she was wearing a silver necklace. "I don't know. Are you sure? How would that even be possible?"

"I don't know," she bit her lip. "But it's her!"

Still unconvinced, he looked at her frantic face. "Let's say it was her, was she a ghost then? Why did she just appear now? What did she want?"

"I wish I knew," Evelyn replied. "Maybe that hole really was going to be her grave and we woke her spirit when we stumbled upon it?"

"Hmm," he said thoughtfully. "You know I don't believe in stuff like this. I mean, come on, ghosts after this long? It sounds a bit unbelievable, don't you think?"

"Honestly, no, I don't think it sounds unbelievable. I don't know how else to explain what I saw."

Greyson pursed his lips, but didn't say anything, still thinking she was hallucinating, but not wanting to invalidate her. "I don't have an explanation either," he finally replied. He turned towards the TV again and they sat in silence, Evelyn on her phone stalking Alyssa's social media page and Greyson lost in his own thoughts.

A little while later, Evelyn turned to him and said, "I think I'll head to bed. Today wore me out. You coming?"

"No, but I won't be far behind you. Get some sleep." He leaned towards her and gave her a goodnight kiss.

She got up and walked to the bedroom, unease starting to creep over her. She pushed it down and got into bed, tightly shutting her eyes, hoping tonight would be better than the last two nights. Shockingly, she didn't have any issues falling asleep. It was when she started dreaming that the real problems began.

Inside the dream, Evelyn tried moving her arms, only to realize she was bound. She heard a male voice call, "You're awake!" He walked towards her with a glass in hand, grabbing a fistful of her hair, forcing the glass to her lips. Evelyn sputtered as the liquid poured down her throat and face. "See, now look what you did," he said as she coughed.

"Please, please just let me go. I won't run. I won't scream. I won't say anything," she heard a strange voice come out of her lips.

The man began pacing. "You're the one that wanted forever, remember?"

"Is that what started this? That one comment?" the voice asked.

He walked up to her, grabbing her hair again, and forced her to kiss him. Evelyn thought she was going to be sick. Her body tried kicking him off her, which caused him to slap her across the face. "Fucking whore!" he spat. "You're rejecting your husband?"

"You stopped being my husband long ago," the voice replied.

He grabbed her by the hair again and slammed her head into the headboard. Tears welled up in Evelyn's eyes, but she couldn't make a sound. "Let's have some real fun now," he said, a wicked smile forming on his lips. He went down on her and aggressively shoved his fingers inside her.

"Drew!" the voice called out in pain. He didn't stop, despite her body trying to kick him off. "Fuck you!"

"Oh, I plan on it," he replied, smirking at her. He took off his pants and thrust inside her, a scream erupting from her lips. "Shut. Up." He exaggerated each word as he put his hands around her throat.

Evelyn began panicking as she realized what he was about to do. Still unable to control her body, she had no choice but to suffer in silence. Her head started spinning as her body was being deprived of oxygen. She felt her eyes close and suddenly her neck was free.

"You're not finished yet. Don't you pass out on me," he said as he continued thrusting.

This vicious cycle continued, occasionally broken by a slap to the face to bring her back to consciousness. Evelyn couldn't take anymore. She wanted this to end. Chest burning from lack of oxygen, she felt her eyes flutter shut once more.

Then suddenly she bolted up and gasped for breath. She felt tears running down her face and moved to wipe them off, realizing she wasn't bound anymore. She started crying thinking about the horrors she just endured.

Her cries and shaking woke Greyson up. He immediately started comforting her, wrapping his arms around her and pulling her close. "Hey, hey, shh, it's okay, it's okay. I got you." He pulled her tighter as if daring anything to come between them. "Talk to me. What happened?" She only cried harder in response. He stroked her hair and noticed a slight flinch when he raised his hand. That was not normal. He moved slowly as to not frighten her and turned her towards him. "Evelyn, you've got to talk to me. You just flinched from my touch. I've got to know what's going on," he pleaded, feeling helpless.

She tried slowing her crying without success; instead she started blubbering words out. "A-Alyssa...he killed her!" She continued crying as Greyson looked on confused. He realized he wasn't going to get a straight answer from her and let her continue until she tired herself out, holding her and stroking her hair the entire time. Once she calmed down, he asked again what happened.

Evelyn took a breath to steady herself. "I saw Alyssa's last moments. I *was* her. It was like I was trapped in her body, not able to move or speak. Oh Greyson, it was horrible. He tortured that poor girl and I felt every disgusting bit of it. I'm horrified. He raped her as he choked the life out of her. He killed her! His own wife!"

Greyson thought she had finally lost it. Surely she couldn't be dreaming about Alyssa's actual death. Evelyn's imagination must have gotten the best of her and concocted this wild story. She immersed herself in this situation far too much. Alyssa's husband couldn't have killed her and then, what? Moved her body then tortured and killed himself? She must have been listening to Jasmine too much. The nightmare explains why she would flinch, but he had to admit to himself that it hurt just a little bit when she did.

"Babe," he said gently. "It was just a nightmare. A horrific, grueling nightmare. It's not real. You're not in danger. No one is going to hurt you." He rubbed his hand up and down her back to try to calm her down even more.

"But-"

"No, Evelyn, listen to me," he tried to find her eyes in the darkness. "You. Are. Safe. No one is going to come after you, no ghosts, no psychotic husbands, nothing."

She looked down, disappointed he didn't believe her. Inside she knew the truth. She knew that Drew killed Alyssa. She lay back down, not wanting to chance falling asleep, but trying to prove to Greyson that she was okay. He frowned and lay next to her, pulling her close again. Though he didn't say anything, he felt the occasional tear land on his arm.

A dark figure moved in the corner of the room, blending in with the shadows, and disappeared.

Neither of them slept the rest of the night – Greyson due to concern for his wife and Evelyn much too afraid to fall asleep. She would intermittently begin sobbing, trying to stifle them as they came on. Though she knew it was only a nightmare, she felt so disgusting, so dirty, so violated. She could still feel Drew's hands on her, well Alyssa. Replaying the nightmare over and over in her head felt like torture, but she couldn't stop it. She couldn't get her mind to focus on anything else. She tried picturing Greyson's smiling face on their wedding day; thought back to her childhood puppy; even tried reliving embarrassing moments from her teenage years, but each time her thoughts jumped back to the nightmare.

The night dragged on until, finally, she saw light begin to filter through the curtains. She breathed a sigh of relief, grateful the night was over. She hoped she could focus on other things now that the sun was rising and briefly contemplated creating a mental chore list, but she needed something to keep her mind busy, too, not just her hands.

Next to her, she heard Greyson sigh. She looked over at him to see his eyes on her, concern on his face. "I'm sorry, I didn't realize you were awake," she said quietly as she sat up.

"I never went back to sleep," he said a little gruffly.

"Oh…" she trailed off, unsure of what to say so she sat there in silence, not meeting his eyes.

"Are you okay?" he asked after a minute of the silence, sitting up, his eyes never leaving her face.

She looked up at him. "No," she finally answered. "I can still feel it. I feel filthy. I feel scared. I feel…" she trailed off again, not quite sure how to describe what else she was feeling.

"I think you need to back off this whole thing. You've gone downhill since we found out and the more you dig into this, the worse you're getting. This is getting to be too much and I can't stand seeing you like this. It isn't good for you." He hoped she understood where he was going with this. She looked down again. "I think maybe you should talk to someone about this. I don't mean family or friends; I mean a professional. Someone who can help you process what's happening."

Still looking down, she replied, "So you think I need therapy."

"Yes, that's exactly what I'm saying, but, babe, it isn't a bad thing. They're available for a reason and this is as good a reason as any. Whether you want to see it or believe it, this is really affecting you."

"It *is* affecting me. Maybe you're right and they can help. I'll do some research online today to see if I can find any in the area who may have availability soon."

"That's my girl," Greyson said as he pulled her in close. He didn't let the tenseness in her body go unnoticed, but didn't comment.

Evelyn got out of the bed and turned on the lights. Greyson shielded his eyes from the offensive brightness. She apologized and gave him a half smile. Now that the sun was starting to shine and the lights chased the shadows away, she was starting to feel a little bit better. Walking through the living room to the kitchen, she turned on every light as she passed. Though she wasn't hungry in the slightest, she began making eggs for Greyson. He wasn't much of a breakfast eater, but he didn't eat much the night before and she figured he'd be hungry. He walked in shortly after she cracked the eggs in the skillet and sat down at the bar.

"Any reason all the lights in the house are on?" he asked, glancing at the illuminated light fixtures in the kitchen, living room, and dining room. She didn't reply. He furrowed his brow. She had been quiet a lot these past few days. Quiet and unsure. Definitely not herself. He hoped the therapy would bring his wife back. Though it had only been a few days, the change in her bothered him and he hated that he was the reason it happened. *If only I had let it go*, he thought to himself. He didn't realize how deep in thought he was until she set a plate in front of him. "Oh. Thank you. What are you eating?"

"I'm not hungry," she replied. He looked up at her, seeing her face in the light. Her eyes were slightly pink and puffy from crying all night. He frowned, but let her be. She cleaned the mess and put everything in the dishwasher then sat down next to him at the bar, laying her head on his shoulder. "So, umm," she started, trying to break the silence, "what are we doing today?"

"I'm thinking today is going to be a pajama day. Since we didn't get much accomplished chore-wise yesterday, I'll put laundry on when I'm finished and sweep while that's going. You can come behind me and mop. By the time we're finished, the laundry should be ready for the dryer. Switch that over and, just like that, we're done for the day. Well, until the laundry needs to be folded and dinner needs to be made."

"Don't forget we need to meal prep. I'm burnt out on sandwiches," she scrunched up her face to further accentuate her displeasure. "I found some simple looking recipes online and I'm pretty sure we have everything in the freezer for pork fried rice."

"Sure. Let's try that out. Though we do need to take out the pork so it can thaw." He stood up and walked to the freezer, stopping to place his dirty dishes in the dishwasher. "Thanks again for the eggs," he called out behind him. Though he didn't turn around to notice, she smiled in response.

They began their chores and just as Greyson predicted, the laundry was finished washing just as she finished up mopping. He switched the damp pile into the dryer and walked back to the living room. "Want to go enjoy the sunshine for a bit?" he suggested.

"Sure," she replied, a little lackluster. "Porch or a blanket in the grass?"

"Your choice," he said, thinking she wouldn't turn down a chance to lay out in the grass. She surprised him when she said they could just sit on the porch. They left their phones inside and went outside for some fresh air.

Evelyn enjoyed the quietness, focusing on the birds flying to and from the oak trees. Greyson, however, was growing increasingly bothered by her silence. He was the first to speak. "Evelyn..." he trailed off, unsure where he was going with this. She turned to look at him. "I love you. You know that don't you?"

"Yes, of course. Why would I question that? Where's this coming from?" Confusion flashed across her face.

"I just wanted to be sure you didn't forget it with everything going on."

"You've been so supportive of me these past few days." She reached out and grabbed his hand. "How could I ever question you?"

He gave her a small smile and squeezed her hand. "So, I've been thinking-"

"That's never a good thing," she interrupted, slightly chuckling.

"Hmph," he replied, but continued. "We aren't getting any younger. Maybe we should try again for kids." Though this had been on his mind for some time, it wasn't where he planned on taking the conversation at this moment, but it worked. Anything to get her talking.

"Wait, what? That came out of left field," she said, slightly stunned.

"Well, it's been a while since..." he didn't finish his sentence. "Maybe things will be different this time. I know how much you wanted kids. I think we're stable enough for this to work."

She didn't expect him to bring up this subject any time soon. Maybe never again after what had happened last time. Neither of them will ever forget the day the doctor told them they lost the baby. She was barely three months pregnant. Her chest tightened and she felt tears prick the edges of her eyes at the thought.

"You really want to try again?" she asked, remembering how broken she felt inside; how much she felt like a failure.

"Only if you're ready," he replied.

The edges of her lips lifted a little as she pictured a toddler bumbling around the front yard, chasing butterflies. "Okay. I'll stop the pill tomorrow." He beamed at her and kissed her hand.

The remainder of the day passed lazily. Greyson folded and put up the laundry while Evelyn cooked the fried rice and portioned it into 10 small containers for their lunch. She was in the middle of cleaning up when he walked back into the kitchen. "What's for dinner?"

She looked up at him and face palmed. She had totally forgotten about dinner, having taste tested as she cooked, she wasn't quite hungry. "I forgot," she said sheepishly. "I'll make something really quick. What do you want?"

"You don't always have to be the one cooking. Let me worry about dinner. Do you want anything?"

"Depends on what it is. I may eat a tiny bit, but I'm not really hungry. I tasted too much while making lunch," she quietly laughed as she sat at the bar.

Greyson wracked his brain trying to come up with something simple that wouldn't make much of a mess that she would eat. It wasn't that she was a picky eater, more that she was particular. While he could eat whatever pretty much whenever, she had certain moods where she wouldn't touch specific foods. "What about chili-cheese fries?" he asked, finally coming up with something that would catch her interest.

Just as he expected, she perked up at the thought, but tried to disguise it. "Yeah, I guess I could eat some of that," she said, trying and failing to hide her enthusiasm. He chuckled and began fixing their dinner.

After dinner and cleaning up, they went to bed together. As Evelyn turned off the lights, the previous night's events came crashing down on her. She froze and began trembling. "Greyson," she called out, unable to move.

"What is it?" he asked looking in her direction, but couldn't see her, his eyes still not adjusted to the dark. She clenched her jaw and forced herself to get into bed. She scooted over to him, but her movements were stiff. His arms wrapped around her, pulling her to him, her body barely moving. "What happened?"

"I'm so scared. I don't want to go to sleep. What if it happens again?"

"I don't have those answers, babe," he frowned in the darkness. "Did you look into therapy?"

"Crap," she said. "I forgot. I'll do it, I promise."

"If it happens again tonight and if you can, try to remember that it's not real. See if you can take control of your dream. Aren't you supposed to be able to have the power to steer the dreams in whatever direction you want?"

"I can't say that I've ever realized I was dreaming in my actual dream," she replied. "So, I doubt that'll happen."

"Okay, that's out then," he paused, thinking for a moment. "Well, if you can't do anything when you're asleep, what about when you're awake? You know nothing like that is happening or is going to happen when you're awake, right?"

"Right."

"So, think of happy thoughts when you're trying to sleep and then when you wake up tell yourself that it was all a dream. I know it's going to be scary when you first wake up, but the sooner you realize it's a dream the better."

She pursed her lips. Sure, it sounded simple enough, but he didn't see it; he didn't feel it. It all seemed so real. Even now, fully awake and aware, she couldn't shake the fear the nightmare brought back. She sighed. "That doesn't help me now, even a full day later, so how is that going to help me as my heart is pounding and I'm covered in sweat, barely awake?"

He thought it over. "I don't know," he finally resolved. "I'm just trying to help."

"I know you are and I really appreciate you." She reached up and kissed his jaw. "We've got work tomorrow. Try to get some sleep."

He pulled her closer and wrapped his legs around hers, completely tangling her in his embrace. She softly smiled in the darkness, but the fear still lingered just below the surface.

Chapter 24

Evelyn had the same nightmare again that night and again she bolted upright crying and covered in sweat. She tried to keep herself quiet as Greyson was still asleep. Shutting her eyes and wrapping her arms around herself, she saw visions of hands reaching towards her. Her eyes snapped open and she jumped.

Her breath hitched as she saw a figure in the darkness by Greyson's side of the bed. All the possibilities ran through her mind in a second. "Get out!" she shouted, startling her husband awake. Her eyes never moved from the spot where it stood, but by the time Greyson sat up and looked around, the figure had faded away.

"What's going on?" he asked, concerned voice thick with sleep.

"There was someone right next to you!" she cried, almost in hysterics as tears streamed down her face.

He quickly turned his head to look around, but saw nothing but empty darkness. "What are you talking about?" He squinted, trying to see in the darkness and gave up, turning on the lamp next to the bed, the brightness temporarily blinding them. He glanced around the room, eyes landing on Evelyn, who still had her arms wrapped around herself and wet cheeks. "There's no one here," he finally said. "Are you sure you didn't dream it?"

She shook her head. "I had that same dream and when I woke up, there it was standing over you!"

Greyson didn't say anything, but looked around the room again. Nothing was out of place; he didn't hear any doors open or close; no one was hurt. Internally sighing, he flipped the covers off and moved to stand up. "I'm going take a look around." He knew she wouldn't have a chance of falling asleep again if he didn't do this for her. Evelyn just tightened her grip around herself as he walked out the door. He returned a few minutes later, shaking his head. "Babe, there's nothing here."

"I don't understand," she said as tears welled up in her eyes again. "Why is this happening?" She began crying again as Greyson sat down and pulled her into his chest, brushing through her hair with his fingers. He sat in silence as she cried, tears staining his shirt. "I'm sorry," she mumbled through the sobs a few minutes later. "You have work tomorrow. Please go back to bed."

"I'm fine right where I'm at," he said, not releasing her as she tried to get out of his arms.

Her crying slowed until it eventually stopped, yet he still held on to her. They sat there together for what felt like an eternity before she spoke. "Thank you," she whispered. He simply squeezed tighter for a moment in response. "Lay down and get some sleep. You've got work."

He didn't say a word, but released her and crawled to his side of the bed. He got under the covers and lifted them, patting the empty spot next to him. Seeing her move towards him, he reached over and shut off the lamp. The room was plunged into darkness again. She cuddled up against him knowing full well she wasn't going to be going back to sleep anytime soon. She just hoped his night wasn't ruined too.

Time slowly ticked by, but Evelyn finally heard her husband's light snores. At least one of them was going to be prepared for tomorrow. She contemplated taking off work, knowing she was going to be utterly exhausted after several relatively sleepless nights. What was she going to do if she took off though? They finished the chores over the weekend and there aren't any pressing house projects she wanted to work on. Her parents live about an hour away, so she could drive out to see them, but that would bring on more questions than she's wanting to answer. She internally sighed. *Looks like I'm stuck going to work*, she thought.

She didn't bother trying to sleep, so she lay with her eyes open, staring off into the darkness. The sun finally started peeking through the curtains, bringing both a sense of relief and dread to Evelyn. While she was relieved for the night to end, she was not looking forward to trying to function throughout the day. Deciding to stay in bed a bit longer to avoid disturbing her husband, she impatiently waited for the alarm to sound. Finally, the alarm started chiming, signaling the end of her wait. She was out of bed before Greyson even sat up.

He looked around until clarity hit him and he realized she must have not slept after the incident last night. He frowned, concerned for her. Their morning passed in relative silence, following the same workday morning routine.

"Don't forget to find a therapist," he reminded her as he gave her a kiss before walking out the door.

"Thanks for the reminder," she called after him.

Evelyn struggled to focus on her commute, her mind totally consumed by the nightmare. She blinked in surprised when she arrived at work, hardly remembering the drive at all. She grabbed her things and walked inside, trying to mentally prepare for the day.

She checked her phone when she sat down and saw a text from Jasmine. *Think I have a stomach bug. Took off today. Hold down the fort!* Evelyn breathed a sigh of relief. As much as she loved Jasmine, she didn't feel up to pretending to be perky today. Though without her, the day would pass by even slower. She replied to Jasmine and got to work.

Just as she predicted, the day dragged on. Every time she looked at the clock thinking at least an hour had passed, it had only been 15 minutes or so. After her morning meetings, she caught up on all the work that had come through over the weekend. By the time her noon lunch break came around she was beyond ready to go home. She heated up her fried rice and went back to her office, gently shutting the door behind her. Calculating her remaining time off, she decided to try to stick out the rest of the day. While she had the vacation, her thoughts circled back to her logic from that morning – if she took off what was she going to do? She sighed again and finished her lunch. Turning back to her computer, she saw that she still had plenty of time and began researching therapists. She found one that was local that had great reviews and called to make an appointment. The soonest they could get her in was in two months. She internally groaned, but booked it, knowing she truly did need the help. She just hoped she could get some sleep by then. Checking the time, she decided to get back to work, but willed the clock to tick just a little bit faster.

Finally, the clock struck five, signaling quitting time. Evelyn packed up and walked to her car, vowing to focus better on her drive home than she did the drive in. She did a little better, but was still distracted. Her spirits brightened slightly as she pulled into the driveway. Home at last.

Quickly changing into comfortable clothes, removing her makeup, and throwing her hair up in a messy bun, she clumsily plopped down on the couch. She lazily scrolled through recipe boards trying to figure out what to cook, not even thinking of tonight's dinner before now. Looks like tonight might be a frozen pizza night. She called Greyson to ask if he was okay with that, which he was, and lay down on the couch. Greyson said he'd probably be home in an hour, so she had time to lounge around.

Without realizing it, she fell asleep. This time she dreamed something different. The woods were peaceful with the sunlight filtering through the canopy of leaves overhead, but it was eerily silent. She was walking through the trees, not knowing where she was headed. Looking around for the path or the bench, anything familiar, she didn't recognize where she was. She was lost. She felt a chill up her spine as she realized her predicament. Her heart pounded as she walked faster, trying to find a way out, leaves crunching beneath her feet. Feeling watched, she stopped and spun around, looking for anyone else out there with her. She saw nothing; heard nothing. She began briskly walking again. After a couple of minutes, she saw a clearing up ahead. Breathing a sigh of relief she headed in that direction.

When she arrived at the clearing, she didn't find the bench, flowers, or lights like she was expecting, but instead a circle of mushrooms. Suddenly mist started to swirl above the mushrooms. Fear gripped Evelyn's heart. A few feet away, more mist appeared. Frozen to the spot, Evelyn could only watch. Two feminine voices seemed to come from the mist. Evelyn tried to listen over her pounding heart. She was only able to catch part of the conversation as the voices seemed to fade in and out, but from what she gathered, she was witnessing two souls communicating. And not just any two souls – the two souls of Drew's dead wives.

Though she was feeling like an intruder by listening in, Evelyn was too engrossed in what was happening in front of her to try to move away. The conversation ended and one of the mists, the one over the mushroom circle, faded away. The remaining mist seemed to take on the form of a woman. Evelyn continued staring. The figure suddenly turned towards her as if noticing her for the first time. Then, without warning, the figure charged towards her, letting out a bloodcurdling scream.

Evelyn bolted up from the sofa, breathing heavily. The smell of pizza greeted her as she realized it was a dream. She looked at the clock and realized she had been asleep for an hour and a half. "Greyson?" she called, sitting up to glance into the kitchen.

"Oh, you're finally awake Sleeping Beauty?" he chuckled, appearing from around the corner.

"I'm sorry, I didn't mean to fall asleep," she said sheepishly.

He reached down and grabbed her hand, "You've had a rough few days and you deserve some rest. I'm just surprised I didn't wake you with all the noise I made!"

She yawned. "Nope, didn't hear a thing. I had another dream."

"A dream or a nightmare?" he asked, wanting clarification to prepare himself for what was to come next.

"Not a nightmare." She went on to recap her dream. While she was talking, the timer for the pizza went off and they walked into the kitchen. Greyson removed dinner and sliced it with a pizza cutter, occasionally nodding his head to show Evelyn he was still listening to her. When she was finished she asked, "So, what do you think?"

"I think you maybe need to really think about this before you go down another rabbit hole. Look what the last one did. Either you're seeing things or a ghost is suddenly haunting you; you're having nightmares; you're a wreck!"

"Greyson, I have to know. It's like Alyssa is showing me these things and I need to see it through," she replied.

"I won't stop you, but please think about it first. I hate seeing you like this." He handed her a plate with a steaming slice of pizza on it.

"Plus, it's affecting my sleep too," he grumbled. They sat at the bar and each took a bite.

"I'm sorry I'm dragging you down into this," she apologized. "I just can't let this go. There's more to this story than the media published and I think Alyssa wants me to find the truth!"

He chewed thoughtfully and swallowed before speaking. "If that's what you believe."

She looked taken aback. "What? You don't believe me?"

"No, no," he said quickly. "I believe what's happening to you, but I don't know how much I believe it's some dead girl's spirit showing you these things. If that were the case, then she should see how much it's affecting you and stop!"

"Maybe she can't," Evelyn said quietly. "Maybe she finally has someone who can help her. Greyson, she might need help crossing over."

He shut his eyes and groaned. "Evelyn..."

"What?" she spat, suddenly defensive. "If you were stuck in the afterlife, wouldn't you want someone to help you?"

"Yes, but-"

"If you were brutally murdered by the one who claimed to love you and the world didn't seem to care, wouldn't you want some form of justice?"

"And how are you supposed to bring her peace? Supposed to help her? Supposed to bring her *justice*?" Greyson was growing frustrated at being hounded. "You're saying her husband did it. Well, if that's the case then he got what he deserved because he's now dead too, in case you forgot. No way to punish a dead guy."

Evelyn was silent for a moment, thinking over what he said. "I have to try," she whispered. "I can't let her – them - just suffer like this."

"Babe, you don't know that she's suffering. You don't know she's the one showing you these things. Hell, you could have just been having nightmares because you saw those pictures and dove too deep into the case. You don't know for sure it's her."

"But, Greyson, I do. I feel it!" she started crying. "I know it's her!"

"Evelyn," he began, gently touching her face. "I'm not saying you can't research this Lily person. I'm just asking you to back off just a little bit. You're becoming obsessed."

She pulled away like she had been slapped, startling Greyson. "Obsessed?" she spat. "Forgive me for just wanting to help people!" She stood up and walked away, leaving most of her dinner untouched. The bedroom door slammed.

Greyson just stared after her. This was *not* normal behavior. Not that she's never flown off the handle before, but never over a small conversation like this. He was getting extremely concerned. Picking up their unfinished dinner, he packed the pizza in a container and put it up. More than anything, he wanted to go in there and comfort her. He wanted to hold her and tell her everything was going to be alright and that he was sorry. But he wasn't sorry. He didn't feel as though he did anything wrong by worrying about her. He may not have worded it the best, but it was still concern for her wellbeing. *Maybe I should apologize anyway*, he thought.

He walked to the bedroom door and gently knocked. "Evelyn?" he called softly. "Can I come in, please?" No answer. He turned the knob – it was open. The room was dark, but he could see her sitting on the edge of the bed, head down looking at the floor. "Evelyn?" No answer again. He walked over and sat next to her.

"Leave me alone," she barely whispered.

"Evelyn I-"

"I said, leave me alone!" She screamed and pushed him, nearly knocking him off the bed.

"Evelyn, what the fuck?" She had never put her hands on him before. "Babe, you've got to calm down. What is going on with you?" She looked up at him with hatred in her eyes, but said nothing. Something wasn't right, that much Greyson knew. He had never seen her act like this before; almost as if she were a different person.

"Get. Out." She stressed each word. Wordlessly, Greyson stood up and left the room. He didn't know what else to do aside from walk out. He would never retaliate and put his hands on her and it seemed useless to try to talk some sense into her. Trying to hold her might end up with more violence. He had to get to the bottom of this.

He sat down on the couch and turned on the TV, not really watching what was playing. He thought about his wife and the changes in her since they found out the history of the home. Nightmares, seeing things or seeing ghosts, obsessiveness, now anger and violence. Was there a connection? There had to be because it couldn't just be from lack of sleep for a couple of days.

He sat there lost in his own thoughts for several hours until he realized the time. Turning off the TV and the lights in the rest of the house, he made his way to the bedroom. Quietly opening the door, he peeked inside, but it was too dark to see anything. He stepped inside and shut the door behind him, careful not to make any noise. Softly walking to the bed, something in the air felt off, but he ignored it and got into bed. His eyes still adjusting to the darkness, he immediately felt, rather than saw, that his wife was not in bed. He looked towards the bathroom and didn't see a light on. He immediately reached over and turned on the lamp.

The room was empty. He noticed the curtains moving slightly though there was no fan in the room. Something about the curtains swaying captured his attention. He got up and walked towards the window. It was open.

Evelyn was gone.

Chapter 25

She breathed deeply and she flexed her fingers. It had been too long since she had a physical body. The nighttime dew clung to her bare feet as she walked towards the woods. She knew the way, not needing anything but the full moon light to guide her. Finding the small clearing easily, she let the solar lights guide her deeper. Reaching the bench, she gently ran her fingers across it. Suddenly she turned and started walking into the trees, not feeling the briars pulling at her skin or the sting of the sticks poking into her feet.

After dodging trees for a couple of minutes, she finally came across an area semi cleared with a perfect mushroom circle in the center. "Lily," she spoke gently. "Lily, are you there?" No answer. Not even a stray breeze.

Alyssa, in Evelyn's body, sighed. She wasn't sure what she expected to happen, but she still wasn't happy with the outcome. Things started to get blurry; she wasn't sure if it was tears of frustration or her power waning. Figuring she should return the body before anything happened to it, she navigated the dark woods with ease. Emerging from the tree line, she walked towards the house, each step becoming more and more of a struggle.

She suddenly fell to her knees. Unable to muster the strength to stand, she slowly slid down to lay on the ground. Giving up, she left Evelyn's body.

"Evelyn!"

Evelyn could hear someone calling her name.

"Evelyn!"

She slightly groaned and opened her eyes. Her body hurt and she was cold – and wet? Sitting up, she looked around her. She was outside. But how did she get out here?

"Evelyn!"

"Greyson?" she called weakly. She wobblily got to her feet and started walking towards the house. "Greyson!"

"Evelyn! I hear you! Where are you?!"

"Walking towards the house," she called, hoping she would be loud enough for him to hear. She saw the beam of a flashlight bobbing around the corner of the house.

Greyson swung the flashlight frantically, trying to find her, eyes darting everywhere. Finally, the light landed on a pale figure in shorts and a t-shirt. He dashed towards her and wrapped his arms around her. "Evelyn, where have you been?!" he exclaimed, still holding her.

"I," she hesitated, "I don't know."

He gently pushed her back to get a good look at her. She was wet from dew and covered in grass. Her legs and feet were scratched and bleeding. "Let's get you inside," he said as he wrapped one arm around her waist. "Can you walk okay?"

"I'll live," she replied, slowly walking forward.

Once they got to the house, she stopped in the foyer and immediately stripped out of her dirty, wet clothes as Greyson ran her a bath. He quietly helped her into the tub and sat on the floor next to her. "Evelyn, I need to know what happened. Where did you go?" He looked at her legs and feet again.

"I don't know. The last thing I remember is we were talking about my dream and then I woke up on the ground, hurting and wet." She quietly swished her hand in the water.

"So, you don't remember the fight?" he asked eyes wide. She shook her head. "You don't remember nearly pushing me off the bed?"

"What?" she asked. "No, I don't remember any of that. Pushing you off the bed?"

"Not important. Did you hit your head at work or something? Anything you can think of that would trigger this memory loss and strange behavior?"

She was thoughtful for a few seconds. "No, nothing happened. No tripping and hitting my head, no falling down the stairs, no car accidents, nothing."

"Maybe we should get you to a real doctor," he said hesitantly.

"Greyson, I'm fine. Okay, I'm a little shaken up, but I'm okay, really."

"Getting violent, escaping through a *window*, and waking up in the grass – all in the middle of the night, mind you – is not like you! Something is clearly wrong!"

Finally feeling warmth throughout her body, Evelyn grabbed some soap and began to lather up. "Didn't you say the other day you thought I was sleepwalking? Maybe it was a case of that, but extreme."

"I doubt it," he said skeptically. "I don't think people go from not sleepwalking to sleep-glaring to whatever the hell you just did tonight. Something's not right!"

She didn't have an answer for him, but knew he was right. What would she say to a doctor? *Help, I went outside and don't remember why or how I got there?* It was ridiculous. Maybe if she had something concrete, she would go. "Just another topic for the therapist, I guess," she said out loud.

"Wait, you found one? When are you going? Where at?"

"In town. But the soonest they could get me in was in two months."

"Two months? Who knows what could happen to you by then!"

"Greyson, what miracles are you expecting them to work, exactly? They're there to help talk through your problems and teach you ways to cope, not magically fix whatever's going on." She opened the drain and stood up. Grabbing a towel, she dried off as he stood up, stiff from sitting on the hard floor. "Could you grab me some more PJs, please?"

He silently walked out of the bathroom and returned a minute later with a fresh t-shirt and panties for her. She thanked him and got dressed as he turned and walked into their bedroom. After shutting the window, he sat on the edge of the bed and waited for her to finish. When she finally stepped out, he patted the bed next to him, signaling her to sit. She did and laid her head against his shoulder.

She looked at the clock and quietly said, "I think I'm taking tomorrow off. I had a hard enough time focusing on the commute today that I don't want to take any chances on the road tomorrow." He stared ahead and didn't say anything, but internally agreed with her decision. She grabbed her phone and typed a quick email to her boss. When she was finished, she looked up at her husband. "Greyson? Say something."

"What do you want me to say?" he asked after a minute. "I'm horribly concerned for my wife. She's been having nightmares that's causing sleeping issues, has been seeing things, might be haunted by a ghost, was violent with me, and now is sleepwalking. All the while I'm sitting here not doing a fucking thing for her, just watching her go downhill. The only person who might be able to help can't see her for two months, so she'll be suffering for two whole months unless she falls asleep on the road and crashes into oncoming traffic or decides to go play with a bear while sleepwalking and-"

Evelyn put her finger to his lips, silencing him. He turned and looked at her. "Hey," she started gently, "I don't have the answers either. But know I'm trying to get help. Know I want this craziness to end, too. I can't go on like this for two months, I know that. I'll be a zombie by then." Her lips twitched, trying to form a small smile. "I'm going to be okay, but you're going to worry yourself into an early grave."

He fully turned towards her and glared. "You're telling me not to worry about you?" he asked incredulously. "I literally just found you outside at night, in the cold, in the wet, bleeding, with no recollection on how you got there or what you did, and you expect me *not to worry*? Seriously?"

Well, when you put it that way, Evelyn thought then said out loud, "You're right. I'm sorry. We're going to figure this out." She reached up and lightly kissed him. "Thank you for always coming to my rescue."

"I'm taking tomorrow off, too. No offense, but I don't trust you enough to leave you alone right now." He grabbed his phone and checked the time. "Plus, it's kinda late." Just remembering she was bleeding earlier, he reached down to pull her leg up on his lap and inspect it. This caused her to lose balance and she fell over backwards on the bed. He smirked and looked at the damage. Nothing major, just a few cuts. He gently rubbed his thumb against one of them. "Do they hurt?"

She looked down at her leg to see what he was talking about. "No, not at all actually. Now my feet, that's a different story. Those hurt, but not like I cut them. More like I stepped on a ton of building blocks or something."

"No telling what you did out there," he said, rubbing her leg. His eyes trailed over her body. He loved seeing her laid out like this, bare leg on his lap. His lips twitched into a sly smirk. "You know, since we're both off tomorrow, we could stay up a little later." He let his hands trail up her body and under her shirt.

She froze.

He felt her body tense and immediately stopped. "What is it?" he asked looking around.

"I-I don't know if I can do this," she said, looking away, face burning with shame.

"What are you talking about? Sex? Why not?" She continued looking away, not wanting to see his questioning eyes. "Let's try?" He softly ran his hand down her calf. She bit her lip, but nodded, still looking away.

He moved her to a more comfortable position and carefully took off her shirt. He trailed his hands up her pale body, followed by gentle kisses. He felt goosebumps form and smiled. Once he reached her face, he turned her to look at him, seeing something strange in her eyes. Attributing it to just her being upset from earlier, he softly kissed her, trying to make her forget what happened.

She didn't immediately open her mouth to meet his, instead pressing it shut in a tight line. He ran his tongue across her lips, asking for permission. Her heart was pounding and felt something bubble up in her chest, but she kissed him back. He wrapped one arm around her back and pulled her body to his, but she gasped in surprise and slightly pulled back.

Not realizing her internal battle, he continued. He released her and trailed his hand to her breast and gently cupped it. A tear slid down her cheek. With his eyes still closed, he moved to take her breast in his mouth. She gasped again as more tears started rolling down her cheeks. Not realizing her gasps were not out of pleasure, he moved to the other breast and lightly ran his tongue over it.

"Please. Please stop," she managed to whisper out.

He opened his eyes and looked up at her tear-stained face. "Oh my god! Evelyn, what's wrong?" Instantly, all traces of the mood disappeared. He quickly handed her the shirt.

She looked away, face red, but still crying. "I'm sorry. I want to. I really do. But I can't!" She began crying harder.

He was torn. Does he reach over and comfort his wife or does he keep the distance she seems to need? He decided to keep his distance, but reached out to place his hand on her knee. She flinched. "Did I do something wrong? What happened? Please talk to me."

She couldn't answer him. How could she tell him that a dream she had was making her afraid of his sensual touch? What sense did that even make? How could she tell him that all she saw was that horrible man's face instead of his?

As if reading her thoughts, he put two and two together. "It was that dream, wasn't it?" His tone more accusatory than he intended. Not missing that, she nodded. "Fucking hell Evelyn. You can't let this ruin your life like you are. What's next, you think I'm going to murder you or something? Fuck."

She flinched, still looking away, not wanting to see the disappointment in his eyes. She knew he was right. This was ruining her life. She couldn't focus, couldn't sleep, suddenly sleepwalks, and is now cringing away from her own husband. She didn't realize she was still crying until she felt him wipe away a tear. She turned to look at him and her heart broke at the defeated look on his face. She grabbed his hand and nearly shouted, "Let's try again? Please? I'll try harder this time. I will!"

He shook his head and pulled his hand away. "No," was all he said as he turned to his side of the bed. As much as he wanted to turn his back to her and be alone in his thoughts, he couldn't bear the thought of her thinking this was completely her fault. In a way it *was* partially on her, but not completely. He opened his arms for her to snuggle inside. She looked at him, silent tears running down her face still, turned off the lamp, and got into his arms. She curled up into his chest and cried until she fell asleep. She was too exhausted to dream.

The next morning, Evelyn awoke to an empty bed. The previous night's events came crashing down on her, taking her breath away. She had to find Greyson and apologize again. She searched the house and front porch, but found nothing. Calling his name proved futile. Didn't he say he was taking off today? He wouldn't just leave without saying something, would he?

She went back inside and checked the sink, only to find an empty coffee mug and a dirty plate and fork. She furrowed her brow and looked around, eyes landing on a piece of paper she overlooked the first couple of times she passed it. She walked over and picked it up.

Got called in to work. Will make it quick. Love you. G.

She sighed. She should have known better than him being able to take off last minute. He didn't have the luxuries she did when it came to time off. Rather, he didn't have the luxuries she did at work, period. While she was pretty much left alone to do her job, Greyson was constantly micromanaged. She didn't know how he could work like that. She would have told the company where to shove it by now if she were him. They were also extremely strict when it came to time off. Shaking her head, she didn't know why she thought he'd be able to stay with her today.

She wrapped her arms around herself, trying to come up with a plan for the day. Drawing a blank, she decided her first course of action would be a shower. That always helps to clear her mind. After her shower, she dressed in a comfortable pair of shorts and one of Greyson's t-shirts.

Grabbing her phone, she made her way into the kitchen to fix breakfast. She sent Greyson a quick text. *Good Morning. I hope your day doesn't suck. I love you.* Knowing she probably wouldn't hear back from him any time soon, she set her phone down and began cooking.

After breakfast, she sat on the couch and drummed her fingers against her knee, careful not to go any lower to avoid tapping on any of her wounds. The bottoms of her feet felt bruised though there were none and her cuts were shallow enough to have completely scabbed over quickly, but not being a massive fan of pain, she was still cautious.

Pursing her lips, she thought about her lack of plans for the day. Then an image of the woods flashed in her mind. She could look for that mushroom circle from her dreams. Surely that would tell her if her dreams were just that or if they really held some truth in them. Confident that would help set things in the right direction, she put on some old shoes and walked outside. Realizing she had no idea where the circle was, she paused once she got to the opening of the trail. She didn't want to just venture into the woods alone, though she did have a wonderful sense of direction.

She thought back to her dream from the other night when she found the circle. She remembered being in the clearing with the bench and facing away from the bench. She walked straight forward, she thought, until she came across the clearing with the mushrooms. Couldn't hurt to try, right? And if she didn't find the mushrooms, she would just turn around and come back to the bench, since she was going straight anyway. Having faith in herself, she stepped forward and down the path.

She quickly made it to the clearing, though she still felt uneasy when glancing at the freshly filled hole. Swallowing hard, she tried not to think of what it could have been used for. She steeled her nerves and turned her back to the bench. Walking forward, she began to expertly slip through the trees, careful of briars. She felt a strange sense of déjà vu. It must have just been from the dream. After all, it was only recently that she had been through this part of the woods in her dream.

She trekked on for several minutes, quickly losing sight of the clearing, but not finding a new one with the mushroom circle. She paused and looked around, suddenly feeling claustrophobic. She turned again and realized she spun herself in a circle and had no idea which way was which. So much for an impeccable sense of direction.

She glanced around. Everything looked the same. A mixture of trees, shrubbery, and briars filled her vision. Suddenly feeling dizzy, she grabbed onto the nearest tree. Her ears started ringing and she felt like she was going to pass out. Slowly getting down to her knees, she continued to hold on to the tree for support.

Evelyn looked straight ahead and thought she saw something white in the distance through the breaks in the tree trunks and shrubs. Ears no longer ringing, she carefully stood up, keeping her eyes on the spot she saw. After breaking through one last barrier of trees, she finally found the mushroom circle. She gasped in amazement at herself.

She walked over and stood near the circle, the images of floating, whispering mist flooding her brain. The realization hit that this may not have been the best idea. She remembered the next part of her dream where the mist charged her and screamed. Suddenly feeling watched, she turned and briskly walked through the trees in the direction she hoped was the trail. After several minutes, she felt as though she should have made it to the clearing by now. She slowed, still feeling eyes on her back, and looked around. Behind her something screamed a loud, bloodcurdling screech.

Evelyn ran. Weaving in and out of the trees, she had no idea where she was going; she just ran. She couldn't tell if she was being chased or if it was her own mad dash through the woods creating all the noises she heard.

Glancing behind her, she should have kept her eyes on her surroundings. She ran right into a fallen tree, smashing her leg and flying over it, landing in a pile of briars. Adrenaline pumping, she tried standing up, but was entangled in the thorny vines. Ripping them off her, she cut her hands, her face, and her arms. Finally freeing herself, she quickly limped forward. Realizing she hadn't heard anything aside from her pounding heart, she slowed and listened, though it was near impossible to hear over the loud thump-thumping. She took deep, intentional breaths trying to slow the pounding. As she was doing that, she looked around. She saw absolutely nothing aside from the same scenery from before. Except now she was completely and utterly lost.

Chapter 26

Lost in the woods with a throbbing leg and no phone, Evelyn tried not to panic. She cursed herself for not bringing her phone with her. She could at least try to figure out the compass app if she had brought it. She looked down at her leg. No bleeding, but she had a feeling it was fractured. If she ever got out of here, she was definitely going to have to go to the doctor.

There were acres of woods surrounding their property and she had no idea how deep – or not - she had ventured. She looked up at the trees, trying to pinpoint the sun as if that would help her. She wanted to scream in frustration. Eyes scanning her surroundings, she saw nothing that would hint at a way out. She sighed and began to limp forward, hoping she was going in a straight line towards the house, the only sound her shoes crunching on the dried forest floor.

She hadn't even put on a watch, so she had no idea what time it was or how long she had been lost, but it felt like hours. With the heavy tree cover, it was impossible to watch the sun, though it was still bright.

Oddly enough, there were no birds chirping or squirrels scurrying. She would have thought these woods would be full of life, but it was still and quiet. Realizing this, she felt a chill run up her spine. Her mind started to race. What if these woods were haunted by Alyssa and Lily? What would she have done if she had seen mist at the mushroom circle? What if she gets stuck here after dark? Will a friendly spirit lead her out or would she be stuck in here until she dies? Panic started to well up in her chest again, but she tried to push it down, knowing panicking would only make things worse.

She continued limping, avoiding briars, spider webs, shrubs, and trees - both standing and fallen this time. Feeling as though she were getting nowhere, she sat on a log and began to cry. She seemed to have been doing that a lot more than usual lately. She thought about Greyson and how upset with her he was going to be when he found out what she did; but she didn't expect it to turn out like this. In hindsight, she didn't know what she expected. How could she navigate through these woods without some sort of guide? It was sheer luck that she found the mushroom circle, but bad luck that she ran away and got lost.

The weight of the past week was too much for her and she began crying harder. She knew she needed to pull herself together and find a way out of this mess, but couldn't stop crying. After she felt like she had no more tears, she wearily stood up and looked around again. She had forgotten which way she was walking. It was hopeless. She had no idea how to get out. She sat down again and put her head in her hands.

"...lyn."

Hearing what she thought was her name, her head snapped up. "Greyson?!" she shouted. Silence. "Greyson!" She stood up and began run-limping again.

"Evelyn..."

She stopped. That wasn't Greyson's voice. It was soft and feminine. She recognized it, but from where? "Who are you?" she called as she spun around, looking for the source of the sound.

"Right," the voice said, seeming to be nowhere and everywhere at once.

Evelyn stood still, unsure of her next move. "Where are you?"

"Right," the voice repeated. So, Evelyn turned right and began walking, eyes frantically searching for anyone in the woods with her. "Straight," the ethereal voice whispered. Evelyn obeyed and continued straight ahead.

"Who are you?" Evelyn asked again, a little more quiet this time. She had a feeling she knew who was speaking, but couldn't believe it. Surely it couldn't be one of the spirits, could it? As expected, she didn't receive an answer. The light was slowly changing, getting noticeably darker than when she entered the woods. Her stomach was doing flips from nerves and fear, but she continued her trek.

Finally, she saw a break in the trees. Once she broke through the tree line, she almost cried again and ran-limped to the house. She saw Greyson's car in the driveway and her heart dropped. She knew she was in trouble, but wondered how long he had been home. Maybe it hadn't been that long and she could play it off...somehow.

He was on the phone, pacing from the kitchen to the living room when she walked in and she knew right then that there was no getting out of this one. He must have heard the door open because his head snapped up, looking in her direction. "She's here, thank God. I gotta go," he said and hung up the phone. He rushed over to her and pulled her into a hug. "Evelyn, where the fuck have you been?" He held her at arm's length and quickly looked her up and down while waiting for an answer.

Eyes puffy from crying and covered in dirt, grass, leaves, and some blood, she looked like an utter mess. "Umm," she stammered and looked away. "I got lost in the woods," she said softly.

"Oh my God, Evelyn, what were you doing in there again?" The frustration in his voice was evident.

She bit her lip, not wanting to respond, but knew this situation wasn't going away any time soon. "I was looking for that mushroom circle from my dream."

"This has got to stop!" He wasn't one to raise his voice, but he had had enough. "You can't keep doing this. Look at you!" Her face burned and she still couldn't meet his gaze. She didn't need to see his expression to know how he looked – brows furrowed, face slightly red from anger, eyes disapproving. She didn't reply; after all, what could she say? Greyson pulled out a dining room chair and fell into it. He moved the one next to him with his foot. "Sit," he commanded. Silently, still not looking at him, she obeyed. "Why?" He didn't have to say more than that – she knew he wanted the full story and she wasn't going to test his patience by only telling half of it.

"I wanted to know if the dreams I've been having are just my imagination or if there's some truth behind them." Her lip quivered. "I figured if I found the mushroom circle, that would prove I'm not just crazy. It would prove that *someone* is making me see all this. Because right now, I feel like I should be in a padded room. I'm having these vivid nightmares about someone else's experiences and it's causing me to fear you. I'm blacking out and waking up places I don't even remember getting to. I'm doing things I don't remember doing. I'm hearing things that I don't know are even there. I'm seeing things that you can't see. Greyson, what's wrong with me? Am I possessed?" If she hadn't cried all her tears already that day, she would have started sobbing again.

Greyson sighed and leaned back in his chair, trying to calm down. "Why didn't you tell me you were going in there? Why didn't you have your phone with you? Why did you think it was a good idea to go alone?" He avoided answering her comment about being crazy as he was starting to wonder that himself.

"I didn't know I was going to get lost in there for hours..." she trailed off, debating telling him how she got out. Would he think to send her straight to the doctor for questioning and tests and not wait on the therapist anymore? Trying to change the subject, she asked, "How long have you been home?"

"Long enough to notice your abnormal disappearance," he replied flatly. "Evelyn, when I saw you left your phone behind, I thought something had happened to you. What am I saying? Something *had* happened to you, but I mean, I thought *someone* had happened to you." Though he was trying to calm down, he was still incredibly upset.

"I'm sorry," she whispered, head still down. "Umm, I think I might have to go to the doctor. I, umm, ran into a tree and my leg is hurting pretty badly."

"Are you serious? Let me see." She lifted her throbbing leg onto his lap. "It's definitely swelling. Do you want to go to the E.R.? They're probably the only place open at this time."

"What about the local urgent care? I'd rather go there than the E.R." She looked up at him and made a disgusted face.

"Okay, urgent care it is. Do you want to change first? No offense, but you look like hell."

She checked the time. "Good idea. Let me go do that while you check what time they close." She stood up and hobbled to the bedroom.

A couple hours later they returned home with Evelyn sporting a leg brace. Not watching where she was going caused a tibia fracture and earned her prescription pain killers and an appointment with an orthopedist. Luckily it wasn't her driving leg, but getting to work was going to require a little more focus now.

Greyson held the front door open for her as she carefully walked up the steps. It was incredibly sweet of him to worry about her like he does - hopefully he wouldn't continue fussing about the incidents that kept happening. She managed to distract him long enough in the car ride that he didn't ask about her little adventure again. She was hoping that subject was over.

"So," he began when they both sat on the couch. She internally groaned, knowing where this conversation was going by his tone. "Tell me again why you were in the woods alone with no cell phone and no way to call for help if you needed it."

She crossed her arms and said, "I told you I was trying to prove I'm not crazy. I didn't know I was going to get so turned around."

"And how exactly did that happen?" he asked, pointing to her fractured leg. "You're not usually so careless," he demanded. Evelyn hesitated, not wanting to go into the details of what she heard. "Evelyn?"

She sighed. "I thought that if I walked a straight line from the bench, I wouldn't get lost. Well, I was walking for a while and finally found the mushrooms," she conveniently left out the part about getting lost the first time. "Before I could figure out what to do next, I heard a scream and I ran. I'm pretty sure I ran in the opposite direction-"

"Naturally," he interjected.

She just rolled her eyes and continued. "*Anyway*. I ran and hit my leg against a fallen tree-"

"And fell," he interrupted again.

Rolling her eyes at him again she said, "Yes. I fell. Want to tell the story for me?" He just held up his hands in surrender. "After that I was obviously lost. I must have walked for hours. I'm actually pretty sure

I walked for hours because of the time it was when I finally got to the house."

"And how did you get out?"

Exactly the question she had hoped to avoid. She could lie and say she just stumbled around until she escaped, but she absolutely hated lying to him. Plus, she was a terrible liar and he'd see right through her. "A voice told me which direction to take," she said coolly.

"A voice," he repeated, voice dripping with sarcasm and skepticism.

"Yes, a voice," she said, slightly irritated.

He leaned away from her to get a better look at her. "So, you're telling me that a voice in your head led you out of the woods you had been trapped in for hours. And I'm just finding out about this because..."

"It wasn't relevant," she replied.

"Not relev- Evelyn, you've lost your damned mind. It's official now." He leaned back against the couch cushion, not sure what to say next.

"So now you think I'm bat-shit crazy," she accused, glaring at him.

"Yes!" He threw his hands up in the air. "What do you want me to do? Lie to you? Tell you, "oh no babe, it's okay, you're not crazy?" No, you've lost your damned mind. You need more than a therapist to help with this. It's beyond that now."

Suddenly her palm flew through the air and landed across his cheek with a loud crack. Out of reflex he grabbed her wrist, but was shocked into silence. "Evelyn...what..."

She yanked her wrist back, cold eyes glaring at him still. She stood up and took a hobbling step towards the bedroom. Turning her head she said coldly, "I think you should sleep on the couch tonight," then walked into the bedroom and slammed the door.

His shock quickly turned to anger. This was the second time she had put her hands on him recently. He stood up and stormed into the bedroom, flinging the door open. He found her in the bathroom brushing her teeth. He stood in the doorway, filling the small space with his physical and emotional presence. She didn't acknowledge him.

When she was finished brushing her teeth, she took her time washing her face. Growing impatient, Greyson grabbed her shoulder and spun her around. "Evelyn! Look at me!" He grabbed her face with one hand and forced her to face him. "Enough is enough! I'm not putting up with that shit. You know I'd never lay a finger on you, but that doesn't mean you can do it to me. Are you even listening?" Evelyn almost looked bored, like she'd rather be anywhere else than there. "What the fuck has gotten into you?" She still didn't reply. He made a sound of disgust, released her, and walked towards the living room, slamming the bedroom door behind him.

Evelyn didn't react. She simply walked to the bed and got under the covers.

On the other side of the house, Greyson was fuming. She's never acted like this in the decade they've been together. Maybe it was the prescription. He grabbed the bottle and started researching the side effects. After some research he concluded that it didn't seem like that should be affecting her – especially not this severely.

He decided to search her symptoms, but most of the results were less than helpful. It seemed as though the sleep deprivation could be a leading factor, but she hadn't lost *that* much sleep. He growled in frustration and tossed his phone to the side.

After a few minutes he grabbed his phone and opened the search engine again. This time he searched for psychiatrists. Luckily, there were several in the area with decent reviews. He looked to see if there were any available appointments, but none had online portals. Diving into a rabbit hole, he eventually found out that she would need a referral and that it could take six months to a year to get in. Sighing, he shut off the screen and put the phone down again. He leaned over and put his head in his hands.

He didn't know if he could do a year of this. He was never going to leave her, but this constant back and forth with her moods, the sudden violent outbursts, these wild ideas she had that left him in a panic trying to find her, the hallucinations. Oh, how could he almost forget, the sleepwalking or whatever was going on. How much longer until something happens and she gets herself seriously injured or worse? What if she has an episode while driving? He couldn't bear the thought of losing her. She was going to the doctor. He wasn't giving her a choice.

CHAPTER 27

The sky overhead was dark with rainclouds. The sound of falling rain filled the air, a soft pitter-patter as the drops fell to the forest floor. Evelyn sat on the bench in the woods, enjoying the serenity of the moment.

She wasn't alone; a woman sat next to her. They sat in silence for several minutes before the other woman spoke. "You know they're all the same, don't you Evelyn?"

Evelyn turned to the woman. "What are you talking about?"

"Men," the woman replied. "They're all the same. As soon as they get an opportunity, they'll take everything from you."

"Not everyone's like that. Greyson's not like that."

The woman scoffed. "He just hasn't had the opportunity."

Evelyn stayed quiet, not wanting to ruin the peace.

"You'll see," the woman said after some time.

"Alyssa, I can't help that you had a bad experience." Evelyn turned towards her and grabbed her hands. "But I can try to help you. Just tell me how."

Alyssa looked away and replied in a whisper, "You can't help me now." She pulled her hands away and folded them on her lap.

"There has to be something! You can't just be miserable your entire existence!"

That struck a nerve and Alyssa snapped her head towards Evelyn. "Do you think I chose this? Do you think this is how I want to be? I should have been living free with a loving husband and a bouncing baby in that house right now! Instead I'm here, stuck in this...existence!" Her voice grew louder and louder, almost at a shriek. Evelyn stood her ground, listening to Alyssa grow more hysterical. Alyssa quickly stood up and paced around the clearing, mumbling to herself. Suddenly, she stopped and turned towards Evelyn. "Just wait until it happens to you," she seethed.

"What?" Taken aback, Evelyn realized how unhinged Alyssa was becoming. She stood up and took a step back. The ground was no longer under her foot and she fell backwards. Landing on her backside, her fear overrode her pain. She quickly glanced at her surroundings and she was in the hole again. She stood up and reached upwards, fingers only a few inches from the top. She jumped, hoping to be able to grab the top and pull herself up, but as she closed her fingers on the edge, the dirt just crumbled and she fell back down.

"One day it will be you," Alyssa's voice said coming from behind her. Evelyn spun around and found herself face to face with a horrifying looking Alyssa. Her hair was floating around her face, her eyes were black, and her skin was so pale it was almost translucent.

Evelyn backed away until she hit the dirt wall behind her. "Alyssa, stop this, please!"

Alyssa screamed and flew towards Evelyn, arms stretched ahead of her. She slammed her hands against Evelyn's throat, pressing her into the dirt wall. She squeezed as Evelyn frantically clawed at Alyssa's arms and kicked where her legs should have been.

None of Evelyn's attacks were working. For some reason she couldn't find Alyssa's legs and it was as if she didn't even feel Evelyn's fingernails scratching at her arms. How was she so strong? Black started to form around Evelyn's vision. Still trying to fight off her attacker, she blinked hard. When she opened her eyes back up again, it wasn't Alyssa with her hands around her throat. It was Greyson. And he had a wicked smile on his face.

Evelyn froze, the black slowly taking over. She opened her mouth to call his name, but no sound came out. She used every bit of strength she had and pushed against his arms, her arms too short to reach his chest. He wouldn't budge. She felt her legs start to sag under her, but Greyson held her upright by her throat.

It was no use. She couldn't fight him. She dropped her arms and let the black take over.

Evelyn opened her eyes to darkness. She had no idea where she was and couldn't tell if she was alone or not. Keeping her breathing steady, she tried to focus on listening. She didn't hear anything or anyone. Things started to come into focus as her eyes adjusted to the lack of light. She realized she was in her bedroom. Clarity began to wash over her as she realized it was all just a dream.

Alyssa was dead. Greyson would never hurt her. *Greyson*. She reached over to touch him, but was met with emptiness. She sat up and turned on the lamp to confirm what she already knew. He wasn't there.

She looked at the clock and frowned. It was a weekday and he should have been in bed. She got out of bed and walked towards the door, not seeing any light come through the cracks. She slowly opened the door and let her eyes adjust. Using the dim light from the lamp in the bedroom, she felt her way around the living room furniture until she found the lamp there. She closed her eyes and clicked it on.

Greyson was laying on the couch, sound asleep. He was covered with the blanket they keep draped over the back and rested his head on his pillow from the bed. She hadn't even noticed it was missing.

She gently shook him. "Hey, babe?" she whispered. "Why don't you come to bed? It's much more comfortable than the couch." He opened his eyes and stared at her, as if not processing what she was saying. She held out her hand to him, hoping he would grab it and follow her into the bedroom. She felt terrible for waking him up, but knew that even as comfortable as the couch is, it couldn't compete with the perfection of their mattress.

He suddenly narrowed his eyes at her and leaned away from her. "Leave me alone," he said, voice thick with sleep, but with a slight edge to it.

Evelyn's jaw dropped slightly. "I'm sorry I woke you, but I just thought you'd be more comfortable in bed."

"What, did you have another nightmare and need me to comfort you?" he spat.

"Greyson...I...No, I just wanted you comfortable."

"I was fine until you woke me up. Now go back to bed and leave me alone." He turned his back towards her.

"Babe-"

"I said leave me alone!" he shouted, voice loud in the silence of the house.

With tears in her eyes, Evelyn turned off the lamp and scurried to the bedroom. She quickly got in bed, turned off that lamp, and began crying.

Neither one had noticed the figure standing in the corner of the living room, watching, waiting.

Now Greyson was awake and typically once he woke up, he had a hard time going back to sleep. He grunted as he readjusted himself on the couch. His eyes passed over the spot where the figure stood, but almost blending in perfectly with the shadows, it stayed out of sight. Greyson muttered something unintelligible to himself.

The figure faded away.

The next morning, Evelyn dragged herself out of bed when her alarm sounded. She hadn't gotten much, if any, sleep since trying to bring Greyson back to bed. She couldn't figure out why he was so grumpy. Sure, she woke him up, but that didn't explain the out-of-character behavior from him.

Not wanting to face him just yet, she decided to break her routine and shower first. Undressing, she looked herself over in the mirror, eyes pausing at the giant bruise that had formed on her shin. Though she was only in slight pain at the moment, she had to remember to bring the pills with her to work. She didn't want to take one and then get on the road until she was sure it wouldn't affect her driving. She continued looking herself over, seeing every cut and every small bruise from her adventure in the woods. Her eyes stopped when she got to her neck. She squinted and got closer to the mirror. Were those faint bruises or was it just the shadows? Evelyn turned her head different ways, trying to determine what the dark spots on her throat were. They weren't going away or moving like shadows would. She gasped as she realized that they actually were bruises. Her thoughts immediately went to the dream from the night before. How could a dream leave physical damage? Involuntarily, her mind flashed to Greyson with his hands around her throat. She quickly dismissed the thought and chastised herself for even thinking it.

Turning on the shower, she looked back in the mirror and continued to inspect her neck. They should be easy enough to cover up with makeup. The last thing she needed was questions when she didn't even have the answers herself. She got in the shower, hoping to wash away the negativity from last night – both her dream and Greyson's attitude.

Finishing up her bathroom routine – hair drying, makeup, hair styling – she stepped back into the bedroom to pick her outfit for the day. Looking at the clock, she sighed and figured it was time to wake Greyson.

To her surprise, when she opened the door, he wasn't on the couch. "Greyson?" she called, but got no answer. Walking through the house in nothing but a towel, she called his name several more times. As she passed the guest bathroom, she felt heat and humidity escaping into the hallway. He must have showered and left while she was in their bathroom. Her heart dropped.

What could have caused this? The last thing she remembered was them sitting on the couch together. She assumed she had fallen asleep and wasn't awake enough to remember walking to the bedroom. But why would he stay behind? It was done on purpose since he came into the bedroom and took his pillow.

A shockwave went through her body. Greyson was in the bedroom last night. He was oddly furious with her. She woke up with marks on her neck. There's no possible way he could have hurt her...is there? Her fingers gently touched her throat, the bruises hidden under several layers of makeup. Alyssa's words from the dream rang in her head. *Just wait until it happens to you.*

She contemplated taking off again, realizing she was not going to be able to focus on work the rest of the day. After all, this time she had an actual excuse with her fractured leg. She decided against it, not wanting to use up all her vacation time and walked back to the bedroom to dress.

She decided to skip breakfast, too upset to eat, but grabbed a cereal bar from the pantry on her way out in case she regretted her decision later. Her commute passed in a blur. When she arrived at work, she decided to text Greyson. *Love you.* She waited a few minutes, but he didn't open the message. Putting her phone away, she grabbed her briefcase and purse and walked inside.

Of course, when she walked in, she was met with questions about her leg. Playing it off, she simply laughed it off and replied that she had tripped. No reason to go into any more details than that. Jasmine was a different story. She wanted more information.

"What did you trip over?" she asked.

"A tree," Evelyn replied coolly.

"A tree. That's not something you hear every day. How did you trip over this tree?"

"With my legs, clearly." Evelyn threw a cheeky grin towards Jasmine, who just rolled her eyes.

"People don't just trip over trees. That's not how it happens. What really went down?" Jasmine kept pressing.

"Jasmine, I'm being serious. I tripped over a tree. I was in the woods, wasn't watching where I was going, and hit a fallen tree. I hit it so hard I fell over. Why would I make this up?"

Jasmine pursed her lips and replied, "Fine. What were you doing in the woods? I thought you had a trail there?"

Evelyn hesitated for a second before she responded. "I was just exploring. Seeing if I could find anything interesting in there."

"I don't get the appeal. It's not like you've never seen trees before."

Evelyn shrugged. "Can't explain it. It's like I'm drawn in."

Jasmine stayed quiet. That sounded vaguely familiar. Didn't Alyssa say the same thing once? She couldn't remember for sure. Not knowing what else to say, she ended the conversation on the guise that she was swamped and walked back to her office.

Evelyn picked up her phone, checking on Greyson's message thread, but he still hadn't read the text. *Maybe he's in a meeting*, she thought. She frowned and decided to get started on her day.

Meanwhile, Greyson was in his company's corporate office working on a report analyzing his progress for the quarter. He should have been finished already, but his mind was elsewhere today. He couldn't shake Evelyn's violent behavior from last night and vaguely remembered her waking him up to go to bed with her. He didn't remember their interaction – that part was an absolute blur, but he woke up on the sofa still, so it must not have been a good one.

He stared blankly at the document on his computer, trying to focus. He sighed and grabbed his coffee mug, deciding to get another cup of coffee. As he walked to the break room, he was stopped by one of the men in the office wanting to chat about the new client. After a few minutes, their conversation ended and Greyson continued to the break room.

There was no one there, luckily. He quickly washed the mug and poured a new cup of coffee.

"Good morning!" a cheery female voice said.

Greyson turned around and greeted her. "Morning Lexi."

She stood next to him and reached over to grab a few sugar packets, letting her hand brush against his. He pulled away and stepped back immediately. Acting as if nothing happened, Lexi emptied the sugar into her mug and poured a cup of coffee. She wanted to say something to him, but knowing he likes his coffee black, she only had a few more seconds to come up with conversation. "I heard you're a top dog now," she said quickly, trying to catch his attention.

He replied, "I wouldn't call it a top dog. I just got lucky with a new client is all."

"A new client that's going to bring this company up up up. You're on a roll, so keep that momentum going." She stepped slightly closer to him.

He noticed everything. How she purposely touched his hand, how close she stands to him, how her voice always gets a little higher pitched, and how she's slightly giggly around him. He made it very clear to her and everyone at the office he was happily married, but it didn't seem to sway her. At least she hadn't made any obvious moves, but maybe it would be better; that way he could shut her down once and for all.

He excused himself and walked back to his office. He sat down and tried to focus on his report again. Yet again, he just couldn't concentrate. Picking up his phone, he saw a text from Evelyn. Slight anxiety filled his chest as he opened it. *Love you.* Those two small words eased the tension and caused him to slightly smile. He replied to her and set down his phone, feeling more ready to take on the day.

Simultaneously, both Evelyn and Greyson looked at their clocks, already wishing it was time to go home.

Chapter 28

Greyson arrived home before his wife. Wondering what kind of mood she was in, he decided to cook breakfast for dinner tonight. He took a pack of bacon and two links of sausage out of the freezer to thaw then made his way to the couch. Half an hour later, the door opened and Evelyn hobbled inside.

"Hey hon," she called to Greyson who had walked to the kitchen to check on the frozen meats.

"Hey babe. How was your day?"

"My leg is killing me. I forgot to bring the painkillers this morning, so that was fun. Aside from that it was a pretty normal day. Spreadsheets, clients, phone calls, interviews, lots of questions about my brace." She rolled her eyes. "What about yours?"

So far so good, he thought. "Lexi is at it again."

"Ugh, seriously? What did she do this time?" She grimaced.

"Not much," he admitted. "Just brushed my hand and decided to stand too close this morning, then decided to try to hang around in my office this afternoon. I don't mind the small talk, but I know how she is. You'd think she'd learn by now."

"Oh, well, let her look, I guess; as long as she doesn't try to touch." Evelyn trusted her husband completely. She never questioned his faithfulness and knew better than to get upset over something so trivial as a woman pining over him. Greyson was a good-looking man, of course he's going to have admirers. So long as they knew their place, Evelyn wasn't going to worry about it. She glanced over at him, his back turned towards her as he mixed biscuit mix together. "Breakfast for dinner?" she asked, wanting to keep the normal conversation going.

"Yep. Figured you'd be happy with that."

"You know it," she grinned. Not wanting to ruin the moment, but needing to talk about it, she hesitantly spoke. "Umm."

There it is he thought as he internally cringed. He knew what was coming.

"What happened last night? Why did you sleep on the sofa and why were you so mean when I asked you to come to bed?"

He froze. Why was *he* so mean? Did she forget her little outburst? "What do you mean why was *I* so mean?" He kept his back to her and forced himself to keep kneading the dough.

"You were practically growling at me when I woke you up," she replied, her voice small.

He thought about his response momentarily. "Why do you think I'd want to sleep next to you after how you acted?"

"How I acted?"

"Yes," he responded curtly. "How you acted. You know, the outburst? The slapping? Ringing a bell?"

"The slapping...Greyson what are you talking about?"

He turned towards her, eyes narrowed. "Don't pretend you don't remember. We were talking about how you've been acting lately and you slapped the shit out of me."

Her face paled as her jaw dropped. "Greyson, all I remember from last night is coming back from urgent care. I fell asleep on the couch and you brought me to bed, didn't you?"

"No, Evelyn, you didn't fall asleep and I didn't bring you to bed. We fought and then you slapped me. Understand why I didn't come to bed now?"

"I-I don't remember any of that. I swear I don't remember any of it. I wouldn't hit you, Greyson!" She put her head in her hands. "I need to go see a doctor. Something's very wrong."

Not trusting her not to freak out on him again, he didn't agree or disagree. He just turned back and began shaping the biscuits.

"I'm sorry," she whispered. "I'm sorry this is happening. I'm sorry I hit you. I'm sorry I don't remember any of it. I'm sorry I don't know how to fix this on my own."

"Just please promise me you'll go to a doctor soon. I'm not leaving you over this, but I don't know how much more I can take. Your mood swings are extreme right now. I never know which version of you I'm going to get. This isn't healthy for either of us." He popped the biscuits in the oven and set the timer. "I was doing some research last night. I think you need to see a psychiatrist, not just a therapist. But you can't just walk in, you've got to be referred. I think it's time you scheduled an appointment with your primary care doctor. They might be able to help get you in and maybe have some answers for you in the meantime."

Evelyn was quiet for a moment. "Okay," she softly agreed. She was fine with therapy because everyone needs a little help sometimes, but the thought of going to a psychiatrist made her nervous. What were they going to find? What if she really was crazy? She clenched her jaw and tried to push the thought out of her head. Grabbing her phone, she logged onto her doctor's portal to schedule an appointment. "I'm able to get in next week," she said.

"I say book it. What do you think?" He replied as he began cutting the bacon into smaller strips.

"I'm willing to try anything that could help. I can't stand the thought of me attacking you like that. Maybe they can give me something or run some tests." She booked the appointment and set her phone down. They didn't speak; only the sound of frying bacon filled the air.

They ate dinner in relative silence, not knowing what to say to each other. After they finished, Evelyn volunteered to clean up, but Greyson shot her down, using her leg as an excuse and sending her to the living room to rest. Instead, she sat at the bar and waited, trying to think of something to say. She wanted to tell him about her dream from last night, but wasn't sure how he'd react.

She finally decided to bring it up. "Umm, babe? I had another nightmare last night."

What a surprise, he thought, but didn't look up. "What happened?"

"I was talking with Alyssa on the bench in the woods."

"Uh huh," he continued wiping down the counter.

"She said wait until it happens to me," Evelyn said quietly.

He looked up at her. "Why would you listen to that? Nothing like that is ever going to happen to you."

"Then she attacked me and she turned into you. You had your hands around my neck and I think I passed out in the dream. When I woke up this morning, there were bruises on my neck."

"What?! Show me," he demanded.

"I covered them up with makeup. Let me go take it off." She stood up and limped to the bathroom to remove her makeup. When she was finished, she returned to the kitchen and walked up to Greyson to show him the marks.

He gently grabbed her jaw and tilted her head to get a better look at her neck. "Evelyn, what the fuck? I swear I didn't touch you." He released her.

"I know you didn't, but I don't have an explanation for this. Is it possible for a dream to bruise you?" She looked up at him in confusion.

"I don't know. I wouldn't think so, but maybe? What other answer is there?" He frowned, looking at her neck again. "Can I see something?" he asked and raised his hand up towards her. She nodded and slightly lifted her chin. He found the finger-shaped marks and placed his fingers there and slowly and gently placed his hand around her neck. The bruises fit his hand perfectly. He paled, removed his hand, and backed away.

"Babe? What is it?"

He looked down at his hands in horror. "You said I was mean last night. What happened?"

"You were just super grumpy. Fussed me for trying to get you to come to bed. I don't remember exactly what you said, but it wasn't friendly."

"So, I didn't touch you, right?"

"No, why? Should you have?"

"Evelyn," he reached up and shakily placed his hand on her neck again. "My fingers fit these bruises exactly."

She put her hand on his arm and gently pulled it away from her. "You didn't do this. How could you even tell? The bruises are so faint."

"I just can. Look, you're not seeing what I am. I swear I didn't do this!"

"Greyson, calm down," she tried soothing him. "I know you didn't. I never said you did."

"But your dream was me."

"My dream was *Alyssa and* you," she corrected. "Alyssa is dead, so do you have an explanation for that, too?"

He looked away, thinking. "No," he finally said.

"Exactly," she said as she grabbed his hand and turned it over, kissing it.

"I don't remember last night. I remember you waking me up, but not what you said, what I said, or even what I did. So, who's to say I didn't do something in my sleep? We were arguing. Granted, I never thought of hurting you during that time, even after you slapped me, but-"

"Greyson," she interrupted. "You. Didn't. Do. It. I know you didn't. There's some other explanation. Can we please just drop it?"

He frowned again, but did as she asked and changed the subject. "Okay, okay. Let's go sit down. I'm sure your leg is hurting. Speaking of which, what did your girl Jasmine have to say about it?"

"She didn't believe me when I told her I tripped. Everyone else took it for face-value, but nope, not Jasmine. She needed to know the full story." Evelyn smiled thinking about how caring her friend was, even if she was a little pushy today.

"What did you tell her?"

"Just that I was exploring the woods, not looking where I was going, and tripped over a fallen tree. Not a lie, just not the entire story."

"She accepted that?"

"Yep. Surprisingly. She did want to know what I was doing in the woods, though." As soon as the words were out of her mouth, she wished she could take them back. She knew Greyson thought the same thing and was not approving of her little visits to that part of their property. She hoped this didn't cause him to bring up the subject again.

"So, about that."

Great, she thought.

"Please promise me you won't go in there alone anymore. Something seems to happen every time those woods are involved. I mean, look what started all of this. We went down that trail and everything's been downhill since. You have nightmares set in the woods. Now look at your neck. You go exploring," he quoted exploring with his fingers in the air, "and break your damned leg! I think those woods are bad news."

"It's not like we can just get rid of them."

"No, but we can stay out of them. We have enough cleared property to have no need to go back in there again."

"But-"

"Evelyn I'm serious. I really don't want you in there again. I don't want either of us in there."

She crossed her arms in defiance. "I'm not a child. You can't just tell me not go to somewhere."

He raised an eyebrow at her and looked at her crossed arms. "I'm not telling, I'm asking."

"Sure sounded like a tell, not an ask, to me," she sulked.

"Why are they suddenly so important to you? What is the alure? You could have cared less before and now you're still obsessed."

"It's not just me." Evelyn looked up at him with slightly teary eyes. "It's Lily. It's Alyssa. I have to get justice for them. I have-"

"Are you talking about the same Alyssa that said wait until it happens to you and tried to strangle you last night?"

"Yes, but-"

"That Alyssa, okay. Just making sure we're on the same page here," he rolled his eyes.

"Maybe I can help her!" Evelyn almost shouted. "Maybe she's stuck here and is frustrated. Wouldn't you be if your lover tortured and killed you and you were stuck in this plane? There's got to be a way to help her move on."

"Why do you feel so responsible for this woman? You have no experience with ghosts, you're clearly extremely affected by this, and you think you somehow have the power to help her move on? When lately you're scared of your own shadow?"

Evelyn scoffed and looked away, but she didn't have an answer for him. He wasn't wrong. She was more jumpy than normal and nearly every night she's dreamed about this situation some way or another. "Maybe I can contact someone. What are those people called? A medium?"

"And tell them what? That a couple died in this house and now the woman is haunting you and you feel responsible for her?"

"No. Maybe. I don't know what I'd tell them. Maybe you don't tell them anything and they just come here and do their mojo and fix everything. I don't know how this works."

"I don't know how it works either, but I doubt it's that simple," he replied gently.

"Can we at least try? Maybe that'll help. Or maybe it won't, who knows. But it can't hurt, right?"

He sighed. "Will you still go to the actual doctor and not put all your faith in this witch doctor you're conjuring up?"

She rolled her eyes at him. "First off, this wouldn't be considered a witch doctor. Second, yes, I'm still going to my real doctor next week. I made that appointment and I plan on sticking with it."

"You have enough time off?" he asked.

"Yes. I made it at the end of the day, so I can just take my lunch then. You know how flexible they are."

He grumbled, wishing his workplace was as lenient as hers. "Okay, fine. But I want to be here when this witch doctor comes. I don't want some crazy person going psycho on you if I'm not around. Or taking you into the woods and using that hole we found for real."

"You're ridiculous," she rolled her eyes again. It wasn't a bad idea though. She had no idea how this type of thing worked and with how things are nowadays, safety in numbers is always better. She snuggled up next to him on the couch, her leg stretched out on a stool in front of her.

They sat in silence and watched the latest episode of one of their favorite cooking competitions. When that was over, she asked Greyson to grab her a pain pill and some water, which he happily did for her. She felt useless, but the throbbing in her leg was too much to ignore. Plus, she still had to walk to the bathroom and shower. It took about half an hour for the medicine to kick in. She felt much better, but kept her leg propped up. After one more episode of the cooking competition, they decided to call it a night and start heading to bed. Evelyn slowly walked to the bathroom while Greyson shut down the front of the house.

After their showers, they got into bed and snuggled up with each other. She wanted to check in on his thoughts, hoping he wasn't still blaming himself for something he couldn't possibly have done, but left it alone and drifted to sleep.

For the first night in days, she had a dreamless sleep.

Chapter 29

The next several days passed without incident. Evelyn's bruises faded and neither of them argued with the other or otherwise fought. She found a medium who was from out of town, but was willing to help and planned on coming by in a couple of weeks. She got in to see an orthopedist to have her leg checked out within a couple of days – turns out she should be using crutches. Everything generally seemed to be going smoothly.

Evelyn eased down on the couch next to Greyson after she arrived home from her visit with the doctor. "So, the primary care appointment went well, I think." She glanced at the clock. It was time for more pain pills. She grabbed the water bottle on the side table and took two.

"Oh?" He turned his attention from the show he was watching to her.

"Yep. She wants me to see a shrink. Fantastic, isn't it?" Evelyn rolled her eyes.

"That is pretty good, though," Greyson said. "It's what you wanted. A referral. What else did she say?"

"She didn't want to prescribe me anything, but told me to keep my therapy appointment and to schedule to see a psychiatrist as soon as possible. Luckily, she was able to pull some strings and get me in to see one within the same network in two weeks."

"Two weeks? That's incredible. Does she believe it's that serious?"

"She has some of the same concerns you do. What if it happens while I'm driving? What if next time is more severe? Even though the episodes stopped for a few days, I know we're all concerned they may start up again."

"At least she's taking you seriously. I like her."

"Me too and I'm glad she was able to get me in so quickly. Now let's bet if I'll come home with wires sticking out of my head for some crazy tests." She laughed at her own joke.

"Hmm," Greyson said, stroking his jaw in mock thought. "Maybe so and just maybe they'll send you home with a straitjacket too. Just in case things get crazy."

Evelyn hmphed. "I don't think I'm that bad," she muttered.

"Oh, come on, don't be so serious. I thought we were playing?" He reached over and brushed her hair out of her face.

She leaned her face into his hand. Without warning, he wrapped his fingers in her hair and pulled her towards him, kissing her deeply. Shocked, she reciprocated then pulled back and gasped for breath. "What was that all about?" she panted.

His eyes sparkled with mischief. "How about we take this into the bedroom?" He waggled his eyebrows at her.

"Umm, hello? This might be kinda difficult." She pointed to her leg in the brace.

He grinned. "Nah. You don't need to do anything but lay there and relax." She rolled her eyes, but stood up and started making her way to the bedroom. Greyson followed her, heart pounding in anticipation. Before she could sit on the bed, he stopped her. "Let's try something a little different tonight and take a shower together first."

"You think that's a good idea? It's a little cramped in there and with my leg-" He took 2 steps and silenced her with another passionate kiss.

He ran his fingers along her body, finding the bottom of her shirt and trailing them along her skin, feeling goosebumps form. He wrapped an arm around her back and pulled her to him, not letting her go. She put her hands around his neck, not breaking the kiss.

He was the first to pull away. "Still think it's a bad idea?"

"No," she breathed. He smirked and led her to the bathroom.

She began taking off her shirt, but he stopped her. Instead, he grabbed the edges and began to slowly pull it upwards, intentionally grazing her abdomen with his nails, knowing it would drive her crazy. He loved to tease her and knowing how impatient she got just added to his excitement. Finally, fully removing her shirt, he expertly unclipped her bra, releasing her breasts. Her exposed nipples hardened. He quickly took off his shirt and pressed her to him, kissing her again. She began fumbling at the button on his pants. He smiled against her mouth and pulled his hips away. "Not yet," he whispered to her, deliberately blowing hot breath against her ear.

He reached down and quickly unbuttoned her pants. Slowly bending down, he trailed his tongue along her body as he slid her pants down. He stood back up and held her steady as she carefully stepped out of them. He took a step back and admired the sight in front of him – his beautiful wife in nothing but her panties waiting for him.

Reaching over, he turned on the shower to heat up the water. She pressed herself against him and kissed him again, feeling his erection push into her belly through his pants. Thinking she was being sly, she reached down to rub against him, only for him to catch her wrist. He quickly grabbed her by the waist, spun her around, pinned her against the wall, and held her captive arm above her head. She gasped and he took the opportunity to seize her mouth. He used his free hand to start exploring her most sensitive region. She groaned as she felt his fingers push aside her panties and brush against her skin.

She tried pulling her hips back, but he had her firmly pinned against the wall. She grabbed a fistful of his hair and pushed him to her, deepening the kiss. As much as he enjoyed it, he wanted to be in control right now. He removed his hand from her panties and grabbed her other wrist, moving it upwards so he could hold both with one hand over her head. She bit her lip, absolutely loving when he got like this. She arched her back, wanting to feel his skin against hers.

The shower sputtered, bringing Evelyn back to reality for a split second. "Greyson," she murmured. "The shower…"

"Let's get in then," he replied, quickly releasing her and removing his pants and boxers. She clumsily took off her panties and got into the shower. He purposefully pressed his penis against her as he passed. "Oops," he flashed her a smile. "Now where were we?" He swiftly grabbed her wrists and held them in one hand behind her back. He pulled her forward slightly so the water could run down her back. He gently grabbed her jaw and pulled her towards him for another kiss.

Trying to wriggle free from his grasp, Evelyn wanted to touch him; wanted to run her fingers along his chest; wanted to feel him in her hand. He held tighter and she slightly moaned as he used his free hand to grab her hair and slightly pull her head backwards, exposing her neck. He planted light kisses along her throat. "Greyson…please," she whimpered.

Releasing her hair, he continued kissing her neck as he reached down to play with her some more. He rubbed her clit, causing a light gasp to escape her lips. He continued rubbing, pulling back from her neck to look at her face. She had her eyes closed and was biting her lip. He stopped and moved his hand up to his mouth. She opened her eyes, wondering why he stopped. He looked her in the eyes, slowly and deliberately licking two fingers, and reached back down. He found her opening and slid his fingers inside of her. She moaned and closed her eyes again. "Look at me," he gently commanded. Opening her eyes, she bit her lip. He began to thrust his fingers in and out of her as she moaned. He rubbed her clit with his thumb, never breaking the rhythm. Though slightly unsteady on her feet, she gyrated her hips against his hand, closing her eyes again. Her breathing got heavier and faster and her moans slightly higher pitched as he continued.

Suddenly he stopped and pulled away from her completely. "What are you-"

"Bathe," he commanded. She quickly lathered her body with soap on the luffa as he watched, silently admiring her. She rinsed and finished, standing under the water, waiting for his next demand. He crooked a finger and she took a small step forward, closing the gap between them. His fingers were suddenly insider her again, quickly thrusting in and out. She gasped and grabbed onto his chest, not expecting this. Just as quickly as he started, he stopped. He smirked and handed her the luffa. Knees weak, she leaned against him and softly rubbed the soap across his chest. She used her other hand to trace patterns in the lather with her fingernails. She began to move her hands down his body. Using one hand to soap him up, she carefully wrapped the other around his cock. He shut his eyes and took a deep breath. She began gently rubbing her fingers up and down his shaft, teasing him. Knowing how bad of a lubricant water is, she stopped and began bending down to take him in her mouth. He quickly stopped her. "You're not doing that with your leg the way it is. Save that for later. Come on, let's get out."

He positioned himself under the stream of water to rinse off and shut the faucet off. He held the shower curtain open for her to exit first. She grabbed a towel and handed him one and they dried off.

Lifting her up bridal-style, he brought her to the bed and shut off the lights. It was still daylight outside and the light seeped through the curtains. He got on top of her, ready to enter her when she stopped him.

"Let me taste you," she begged. How could he say no to those begging eyes? He turned to his side of the bed and waited. She positioned herself so she wouldn't hurt her leg and leaned down. She didn't take all of him in her mouth at once, instead running her tongue around the tip. Trailing her tongue down the shaft, she found a vein and followed it back up to the tip. He gasped as she gently wrapped her hand around him and put him in her mouth. She trailed her tongue around the tip as her hand slowly moved up and down. He squirmed under her touch. She released him and repositioned herself. Opening a little wider, she took him all the way down to the base. He moaned loudly, not expecting that from her. She trailed her tongue along the side as she raised her head.

"Please," he moaned. "Let me have you. I can't take it anymore."

"All yours, babe," she breathed. He moved and positioned himself above her. Then entered her and thrust deep inside her. She moaned and arched her back. He began quickly thrusting, moaning her name. He bent down to kiss her, his breathing ragged. She bit his lip, causing him to moan again and push harder into her. She tried moving in rhythm with him, but in her current position she felt a piercing pain in her leg and stopped, allowing him to have all the power. He could feel his pleasure building.

Despite the slight pain in her leg, the pleasure overtook her and she loudly moaned his name. That pushed him over the edge and they finished together. Once he rolled off her, a smile spread across his face and he gently grabbed her and kissed her. He opened his arms for her to nestle inside.

After some time, they got up and dressed, both hungry after their little escapade. Evelyn sat at the bar while Greyson heated up leftovers for them. They ate in pleasant silence until Greyson spoke up. "By the way; Lexi again."

Evelyn looked up at him and rolled her eyes. "Ugh. What now?"

"This time she got a little too close in my office. Leaned all over my desk, put her hand on my shoulder when she was looking at the computer screen, extra friendly conversation."

"Does she do this with anyone else?"

"Well, no and that's the problem. I think it's getting out of hand. It's minor stuff and it could be harmless, but I'm not a fan of it. I don't want to say anything to her and have things get awkward at the workplace. I'd rather not go to HR because I don't think it's that bad."

"So, do you just ignore it?" she asked.

"I don't know what to do. I don't want this to continue."

"Have you stopped her while she's doing it?"

"Like I said, I haven't directly said anything, but I shrugged her off after she left her hand on my shoulder and moved as far away as I could while she was on my desk. I've stopped being friendly with her and am short. I feel rude doing it, but I can't have her thinking something is going to happen between us." He sighed.

"Maybe you need to remind her you're married?" Evelyn suggested.

"I don't think it'll help. She knows already. I wear my wedding ring. I mention you often. Just doesn't seem like she's the type to care."

Greyson was always observant, something she absolutely adored about him. Evelyn wasn't the type to get jealous and she didn't want to meddle in Greyson's business. She knew he could handle this on his own; he just had to find a method that he was comfortable with. "I really appreciate you telling me whenever she does something," she told him.

"Why wouldn't I?" he asked, puzzled. "It's not like I want to keep this a secret. Hell, if anything, I want your advice on how to get rid of her. You're a woman, you know how women think."

Evelyn laughed. "That's not how it works, babe."

"Should be," he grumbled.

After dinner and cleaning up, they made their way to the couch to relax. Time passed slowly as they enjoyed each other's company, watching game shows with a little playful competition and banter filling the air. When it was finally time for bed, they went together and fell asleep with their bodies intertwined.

Chapter 30

The next several workdays passed without incident. Things seemed to be going well for the Reeds. The weekend came and Evelyn had just one request for Greyson.

"Hey, hon?" Evelyn asked, turning her head to look at him while they were cleaning up the front garden.

"Mhm?" he acknowledged her while pulling weeds.

Evelyn hesitated, knowing full well how he was going to react. She had to try. "I've been thinking about the woods again."

Greyson froze mid pull. He turned to look at her. "I know you're not serious."

She bit her lip and looked away. "I can't help it. It's like they're calling me."

"I thought you were done with that?" he asked, wiping his hands on his pants.

"I don't know. I thought I was, too. But I keep having dreams and-"

"What dreams?" he demanded, interrupting her.

"Nothing serious!" she quickly clarified. "Just dreams where I'm wondering through them. Nothing's chasing me. Nothing is after me. It's calm and peaceful. Greyson, I want to open up the trail again."

"No," he said with finality. "You've stayed out of there and you've been perfectly fine. You haven't had any episodes, no nightmares, nothing. You're done in there."

She narrowed her eyes at him and said, "Don't you dare treat me like a child."

"It's not treating you like a child," he argued. "It's keeping you safe. Listen, I don't like telling you that you can't do things. Hell, do I ever tell you that you can't do something? No. But this is where I draw the line. You're not going back in there and that's that."

She tossed the loppers to the side and stormed back into the house as fast as she could manage with the brace on. Slamming the front door, she grumbled to herself and walked to the kitchen. She washed her hands and walked to the bathroom to change into clean clothes. Deciding to shower to rinse the dirt off herself first, she reached behind the shower curtain to turn on the water then stripped. Opening the curtain and looking down to step over the edge of the tub, she saw a mangled man slumped over in their tub. His head was rolled to the side. His face was a bright, blistered red, and several deep wounds oozed blood. Red splatters dotted the walls. She screamed and hobbled to the front of the house. Throwing the front door open, she screamed Greyson's name.

He immediately jumped up and ran to her. "What's wrong?"

She pointed to the bathroom and fumbled out, "There's someone in the bathroom!"

Greyson quickly ran to the bathroom as Evelyn stayed behind in the kitchen. Realizing she was naked, she suddenly felt incredibly self-conscious. Her eyes darted around, looking for any bit of movement. She heard the squeak of the faucet turning off and a few minutes later, Greyson emerged from the bedroom confused. "Evelyn, there's no one there. I checked the bathroom and the bedroom. The bedroom window was closed and still locked. There was no one in the closet. The underneath of the bed is so full of crap that no one could fit under there. Are you sure you saw someone?"

"I swear there was someone in there. He was slumped over and there was blood on the walls and in the tub. He looked dead!"

"Unless he was a zombie, I don't think there was anyone there. There was no blood, no wet marks like someone got out of the running water, and no body. Are you sure you didn't imagine it?"

"Greyson," she said, her voice rising a pitch. "There was a man in the bathroom. I didn't imagine it. Oh my God." Evelyn began shaking and wrapped her arms around herself. "What if it's another ghost? I swear I'm not crazy."

He wrapped his arms around her and pet her hair. "I didn't say you were," he said gently. "Come on, let's go shower." Their previous argument forgotten, he led her to the bathroom. She hesitated walking through the doorway. He put his hand on the small of her back and gently pushed her inside. Her eyes wide, she stared at the empty tub.

She started crying. "Greyson, he was right there." She pointed to the tub. "I saw him, his blood, everything!"

Worrying this was a sign of her episodes starting up again, Greyson pulled her close. "Shh," he said as he gently rocked her. "I've got you. No one is going to hurt you." He released her and walked to the shower, closing the curtain and turning the water on again. He got undressed and stepped inside, holding out his hand for her to join him. She hesitated, but took his hand and stepped in.

They showered and afterwards he helped her dry off, dress, and put her leg brace back on. He led her to the living room and sat her on the couch. Sitting next to her, he put his arm around her shoulder. "Are you okay?" he finally asked.

She buried her head in her hands. This couldn't be starting up again. She was doing so well. She hadn't had an episode in a week. No hallucinations, no ghosts, no nightmares, no blacking out and waking up in strange places. Nothing unusual. Now this? Squeezing her eyes shut, she held back tears. She wasn't going to cry. She felt Greyson adjust his arm and turn her towards him. Head still in her hands, she didn't look up. He put both arms around her and pulled her closer.

"It's okay," he whispered. "We're going to figure this out together." Though he wouldn't say it out loud, he was grateful her psychiatrist appointment was soon. Hopefully they had answers. *It's those fucking woods*, he thought. *As soon as she brought it up, this happened.* He narrowed his eyes at the thought. How he wished he could burn them down and erase every trace. Knowing it would never happen, he resolved himself to do everything in his power to prevent her from going there again. He felt Evelyn tense in his arms. "What is it?" he asked.

Evelyn didn't say anything, but released her head and stared blankly ahead. Flashes of the man's burnt face ran through her mind. Realizing she would probably have nightmares tonight, an uneasy feeling welled up in her chest. Though she had hours until it was time for bed, she was already dreading it. She blinked and forcing a smile, turned to Greyson. "I'm okay."

He gave her a look. Though he knew better than to believe her, he kept silent, not wanting to rock the boat. He just held onto her as she put her head on his shoulder.

A few minutes later, she wriggled free from his grasp and looked at him. "I think I want cookies for dessert," she declared.

"Well, that was random," he chuckled. He had hoped this meant she was fine, but wasn't going to hold his breath. "Okay, we'll make cookies after dinner."

She grinned, trying to distract herself. They sat together for a while longer before Evelyn got bored. Trying not to think of the man she saw, she stood up and stretched. "I'm going outside again. Are you coming?"

"Yeah, I'll come," he answered. "But you're not doing anything this time. Just sitting on the porch, okay?"

She rolled her eyes at him. "Fine."

They made their way to the porch and sat in the rocking chairs. A woodpecker sounded somewhere in the distance. Songbirds chirped and flew from oak tree to oak tree. The occasional squirrel scurried across the expansive branches.

Evelyn was getting restless. "Greyson, I need to do something," she said as she turned to him. "I'm way too bored."

"What do you want to do?" he asked tilting his head.

She huffed. "That's the thing, I don't know. I don't feel like shopping. I don't feel like chores. I don't know what I want to do, but sitting here like a bump on a log isn't it."

"Okay," he pursed his lips, thinking. "What about a new hobby?"

"Like what?" she asked.

"Umm. You could take up crocheting," he gave her a cheeky grin.

"Boring. Next."

"Cooking?"

"Don't I cook already?" She gave him a face.

"Biking?" She glanced around at the meadow and woods surrounding their house and back at him. "Okay, that's out. Archery?" She shook her head. "Gaming?"

"Like video games?"

"Yeah, video games. It's something we could do together or each of us could do alone. There are so many options. We could even try out the virtual reality stuff."

"Sounds like the best option you've had so far," she admitted. "But I don't know if that's quite it, though."

"Fishing? Yoga? Drawing? Painting? Playing an instrument? Gardening?"

Evelyn gasped. "Gardening! You know how much I love plants. Let's build an herb and veggie garden!"

"Let's?" he repeated. "As in us? When did this turn into my hobby?" he chuckled.

"You know I can't execute my ideas on my own. They're usually too grandeur." She looked up at him with puppy-dog eyes.

He rolled his eyes, "Fine. But we have to wait until your leg is healed, deal?"

She squealed in excitement and clapped her hands. "It's a date! Come on leg, hurry up and heal!"

He laughed at her. "Maybe you should do some research on what types of plants will grow here while you're waiting. The, what is it called, growing zone or something? And don't different plants grow in different seasons? You should be healed up in eightish weeks total, so as long as you don't do anything stupid, we can start then. In the meantime, do some research on the plants and work up some blueprints for this garden. Do you want it raised, big or small, in the ground, weed barriers, covered, trellises, what?" Evelyn just stared at him. "What?" he asked.

"Nothing. I'm just excited you seem into this. I didn't expect that kind of reaction out of you is all."

"Why not? It's something you seem interested in and we can do it together, so..." he trailed off.

"I love you," she said, smiling at him.

His heart swelled. "Love you too, babe."

Eager to start her research, Evelyn hobbled inside to grab her phone and a notebook. Smiling at her enthusiasm, Greyson just turned his head to admire the tranquility surrounding them, happy the fear from her incident seemed to have faded.

For the rest of the evening, Evelyn talked on and off about what she was finding in her research. Different types of vegetables and herbs that thrived in this environment, various garden plans she found online, which one she thought would work best, how long it would take to build, and the seasonality of different plants.

Greyson brought up a greenhouse since winters in Minnesota got brutal. They both started researching that and quickly realized they may be in over their heads if they wanted to grow year-round outdoors. They opted for a greenhouse for spring through fall growing, leaving the brutal winter as a break and planning season for the following year.

This may be more of an undertaking than either of them initially thought. After taking several pages of notes, Evelyn put her phone down and sighed. "There's just so much information. This isn't as easy as I thought it would be.

Greyson thought for a moment and agreed. "Maybe we can save up until next spring, plan everything out step-by-step, and be ready to tackle it the moment the last frost is gone. Sound like a plan to you?"

"I guess," she sighed. While she was incredibly excited for this new project, she needed something fulfilling right now. "This doesn't solve my problem right now, though. I'm still bored."

"I can figure out a few ways to keep you entertained," he said, waggling his eyebrows.

She playfully pushed him and called him a pervert. He just laughed and wrapped his arm around her shoulders. She had all but forgotten the earlier incident.

Chapter 31

The events from earlier came crashing down on Evelyn as soon as she walked into the bathroom to brush her teeth. She froze in the doorway and quickly looked over to the tub, expecting to see the bloody man there. She let out a breath she didn't even know she had been holding when she saw the tub was empty.

After too quickly brushing her teeth, she skipped flossing and brushing her hair for the night and quickly walked to bed. Greyson was already there, facing the other way, fiddling with the lamp on his nightstand. "Temperamental thing," he said as he stood up and unplugged it. "We need new lamps. This one doesn't always like to turn off and I'd prefer not to get electrocuted when trying to turn it off one day." He turned to look at her and saw the fear on her face. "What's wrong?"

She swallowed. "I had kinda forgotten about the man I saw. I remembered when I went in there and now I'm afraid." She felt silly admitting it, but couldn't help the truth.

I was afraid of that, Greyson thought. He just opened his arms for her to crawl into and held her close. "Turn off the light. I've got you." He loosened his grip and she leaned over to shut off her lamp. Quickly snuggling back into his arms, she wrapped her arm around one of his, holding onto him tightly. Feeling ridiculous again, she took a deep breath and eased her grip on his arm.

It didn't take long for Greyson to fall asleep and Evelyn wasn't too far behind him, though she knew what awaited her. Just as she expected, she had nightmares all night. When her alarm slowly dragged her out of her latest one, she gratefully opened her eyes only to come face-to-face with a man staring at her. He was crouched next to her side of the bed. He had a red, blistered face freckled with blood. His eyes were wild and he wore a horrifying grin. Blood was coming from his mouth, dripping down his chin. She jumped back and screamed, causing Greyson to shoot up. "What is it?!" he demanded.

Now hyperventilating, Evelyn stuttered out, "He-he was here! He was looking at me!"

"Who, Evelyn?"

"The man!" she cried. "He was in the bedroom, leaning over me. Oh, Greyson, he was horrible looking. He had burns all over his face and he was covered in blood. He had this-this awful grin on his face." She stopped to gasp for breath.

Greyson almost face palmed. *Here we go again*, he thought. "Evelyn, baby, shh. It was a dream. There's no one here. I promise."

"But, Greyson, *he was here*. I'm not imagining this! I saw him! It was the same guy from the tub! I think it's Drew!"

"How do you know? Did you see the guy in the tub's face?" He had to keep her talking.

She breathed heavily, but seemed to be calming down. "No, but-"

"Then you don't know it was him."

"But who else could it be?"

Greyson didn't have an answer for her, so he grabbed her and held onto her instead. "You're okay. You're okay." He felt hot tears hitting his arm and started gently rocking her, stroking her head. He just realized her alarm was still playing. "It's Sunday, isn't it?" he asked confused. He felt her nod as he reached over and shut the alarm off. "Why did you set an alarm for today?"

She mumbled something he couldn't understand. Something about a nightmare. He internally shrugged and continued holding her, knowing she'd talk about it when she was ready. Wanting to keep her talking, but not wanting her to relive her nightmare or what just happened, he asked about one of her favorite topics: food. "What do you want for breakfast this morning?" he asked, his tone light, but slightly strained.

"I'm not hungry," she muttered.

"What if I made your favorite?" He felt her slightly shift, her body giving away her interest.

"Cinnamon rolls?" she asked hopefully.

"Cinnamon rolls," he confirmed. *Bingo*. He felt her nod and released her. "Are you okay enough for us to go into the kitchen?" She nodded again. "Come on. Get up and let's go," he said softly.

Clinging onto his arm, she fumbled with the covers and slid over to the edge of the bed. Letting go, she stood up and turned to look for him. He hurried to her side and she attached herself to him again. *This is going to be a day,* he thought as they slowly made their way to the kitchen. He sat her on a barstool and got to work on the cinnamon rolls.

Forty minutes later, he was pulling the piping hot pan out of the oven. Evelyn loudly smacked her lips in anticipation as Greyson slathered the cream cheese frosting over the top. "Smells amazing, hon," she said as he placed a plate with two of the steaming pastries in front of her. Not waiting for it to cool, and regretting her decision as she burned the roof of her mouth, she quickly tore off a piece, chewed, and swallowed, then immediately took a sip of cold chocolate milk. "My compliments to the chef," she gave him a wink.

"I don't know how you even tasted it with as hot as they are," he said, fanning his own plate to cool them off, growing a little impatient himself.

She finished unrolling one and broke off another piece, letting it cool slightly before popping it in her mouth. "Talent," she said, mouth full.

He rolled his eyes at her, but smiled, happy to see her mood improved from earlier. He took a bite out of his and raised his eyebrows. "These *are* good!"

"Told you," she replied, popping another piece in her mouth. "I could eat these all day, every day."

"Doubt it," he laughed. "You'd get so sick and tired of them and you know it."

"Nah," she said and tossed him a grin. "Try me."

"You'd like that way too much," he chuckled. They continued eating, playfully bantering back and forth. When they were finished, Greyson told her to stay put while he cleaned up and put away the leftovers. "Surprised you left any behind," he teased.

"Want me to eat them all? Because I totally can," she shot back smiling.

"Oh, please, be my guest," he bowed and handed her the container.

She merely ran her finger across one, grabbing some frosting, and licked it off. She pushed the container back towards him and grinned. "Saving the rest for later."

Greyson was ecstatic to see her smiling as much as she was. He didn't expect something as simple as cinnamon rolls to improve her mood this drastically. Hoping this would last, he asked her what she wanted to do today.

"Hmm," she said as she pursed her lips. "I'd love to start on the garden-" Greyson shot her a look and she held up her hands in mock surrender. "*But* I know you won't let me. I don't know. What about you? What do you want to do?"

He hadn't really made any plans, but he didn't feel like sitting around the house either. "What if we visited your parents?" He loved his in-laws. Having lost his own parents, he sometimes longed for the feeling of family again. Not that his wife wasn't family, but something that she couldn't provide.

"Sure," she said brightly. "Let me text Mom." She hopped off the barstool and walked over to the bedroom then froze.

There he was again. He had his back to her, facing the bed. He turned his head, his familiar face covered in raw, red burns, and stared at her. A gruesome smile slowly spread across his mangled face, stretching a bit too wide. He turned his body and took a step towards her.

She screamed and backpedaled so hard she fell over. Greyson rushed over and looked into the bedroom, but saw nothing. "Evelyn!" He grabbed her shoulders and pulled her towards him.

"He's in there!" she shrieked, cowering away from the bedroom.

Greyson immediately stood up and dashed into the bedroom. He looked everywhere – the closet, under the bed, behind the curtains, in the bathroom – but found nothing.

Evelyn had been watching his every move while her eyes simultaneously darted around the room, looking for the burnt man. He had just disappeared - again. "Greyson, I swear…"

"I believe you," he said, crouching down to her level and wrapping his arms around her again. He wholeheartedly believed she saw someone, just probably not a *living* someone. She looked up at him with fear in her eyes. He hated seeing her hopeless like this. Everything in him wanted to console her, to hold her, to take away her pain and fears. He just didn't know how to do that anymore. All the progress this morning had disappeared. Silently, he counted the days until her psychiatry appointment. *Eight more days of this.*

Evelyn knew he thought she was losing her mind. Hell, she thought she was losing her mind. She had been doing so well; what happened? Nothing changed. She didn't go into the woods. She didn't...oh. She talked about the woods. Surely that can't be what started all this, but what other explanation is there? Was this her own fault? Has she been bringing this upon herself? She realized Greyson was talking to her, but couldn't make out what he was saying. She was trying to focus, but everything was foggy. Suddenly, everything went black.

CHAPTER 32

Evelyn awoke to someone slapping her across the face. Her eyelids snapped open, eyes searching for her assaulter. She saw a figure standing in front of her, but her vision was blurry. She felt hot tears falling down her cheeks. She blinked hard, trying to clear her eyes and tried moving her hands to wipe away the tears, but found she couldn't move. Hearing a sound that seemed vaguely like a voice, but unable to discern it, she struggled to listen. Unable to move, unable to hear, and unable to see, panic welled up in her chest. Her vision and hearing gradually returned and she heard a voice coming into focus.

"...see." She scanned her surroundings as she tried to focus on what the voice was saying. A man came into view. A horribly disfigured, mangled man. She gasped as recognition hit her. It was the man in her bedroom and bathroom! It was Drew! He grabbed her by the hair and lifted her from the ground. She tried screaming, but no sound came out. A cruel laughter rang throughout the air as he dropped her, her body crumpling underneath her. Her ears rang as her head hit the ground.

Still unable to move, Evelyn tried processing where she was. She was able to focus enough to see they were surrounded by trees and she assumed she was laying on the forest floor. The ground underneath her felt both crunchy from dried leaves and wet from...rain? Was it raining? She wasn't sure. Shifting her eyes to find the man, she saw a large dirt pile.

"It's almost winter, love," the man said from somewhere outside her vision. "They'll never find you. Soon the ground will freeze and it'll be all over. Come spring, you'll be nothing more than a memory." He walked into her line of sight and looked down at her, a too wide smile filling his horrible, blistered face.

She wanted to retort. She wanted to scream. She wanted to run. But she lay there paralyzed, unable to do anything except listen to his taunts. He walked out of sight again. Feeling was slowly coming back into her limbs and she felt binds biting into her wrists and ankles. Her head started to throb. She tried squirming, but despite starting to feel pain again, she was still incapable of movement. Suddenly she felt her body being dragged. She yelped in surprise, but once again, no sound escaped her lips.

The man lifted her with ease and she was able to get a better view of her surroundings. They were in the clearing with the bench and something she's seen so many times – a large hole. He walked over to the hole and rearranged her in his arms, now holding her by the shoulders and letting her feet dangle. He gently lowered her into the hole with strength a man his size shouldn't possess. Leaning down, but staying out of the hole, he released her, her body falling the rest of the way in. Though the fall wasn't far after he lowered her in, pain shot through her body as she landed on her back, her head once again hitting the ground.

The man walked out of view and began talking to himself, uttering what seemed to be nonsense Evelyn couldn't follow. She looked up at the sky trying to gauge how deep the hole was. She must be four feet under the surface. Without warning, dirt began flying over her more quickly than she thought possible. She started hyperventilating, but her body wouldn't cooperate and breathe properly. She felt like she was suffocating. Trying to calm herself down, she realized panicking would do her no good in this situation. She had to think of a plan fast.

More dirt rained down on top of her as realization hit: He was burying her alive.

Evelyn could do nothing but watch as the dirt slowly piled on top of her. Every now and then, he would peer over the edge as if admiring his work. He was sure to leave her head exposed, making eye contact every time he looked over at her - horrifying eye contact with eyes glinting with malice. She was terrified.

The weight was slowly getting heavier on her chest, making it even more difficult to breathe. She felt inexplicably claustrophobic, no longer numb to everything, but unable to free herself from the bindings or the crushing weight of the dirt.

It started raining harder, which caused the dirt that was piled up on her chest and around her shoulders to fall into her mouth and face. She began coughing by reflex, which only made things worse. She tried catching her breath, but could only breathe in short gasps. She didn't notice Drew standing over the edge watching curiously as she struggled.

Her chest was tight. Her body felt heavy. Her throat burned from gasping so much, yet the man began again. She didn't know how much more of this she could take. The pain was almost unbearable. She felt tears falling down her cheeks, mingling with the rain. All of a sudden she felt more weight on her legs. Frantically blinking to clear the tears and looking around, she saw that Drew had gotten into the hole with her and was standing at the edge by her feet.

Glancing around at his handiwork before turning his gaze to her. "You were a lot easier than I expected, Evelyn. You didn't put up a fight. You didn't struggle. You just let whatever was going to happen,

happen. I like that about you." He gave her a wink. She shuddered internally. "Well," he said hopping out of the hole, "I better get back to work. I'd like to finish up before dark. What do you think, Greyson?"

Greyson?! Her mind was instantly clear. She tried shouting his name, but she couldn't find her voice. Eyes frantically searching for him, she finally saw his face look over the edge. Stepping forward and looking down at her, he gave her a disgusted look. There was a woman standing next to him, hands on his chest. She turned her head to look at Evelyn with a smirk on her face. He wrapped his arm around her waist as he said, "Finish the job. I'm tired of dealing with this."

Evelyn's heart sank. She couldn't have heard that right. There's no way Greyson would ever betray her. She tried calling his name as he turned his back towards her and walked away. Suddenly able to move, she struggled with all her might, but even if she wasn't bound, the weight of the dirt was just too much. She was trapped.

Dirt began falling on her face at an alarming pace as the man quickly continued his job. Instinctively, she let out a scream; a sound so loud it echoed throughout the trees. The movement caused more dirt to fall in her mouth and she began gagging and choking. She let out one more scream before her voice became muffled: "Greyson!"

She couldn't hear his footsteps crunch on the fallen leaves as he walked away.

Chapter 33

Evelyn's eyes fluttered open. She found herself in a bright white room; there was a slow, rhythmic beeping in the background. She groaned and tried to move, but found herself pulling against wires on her arms.

Racking her foggy brain trying to remember how she got here, clarity suddenly hit as she remembered being buried alive. Frantically looking around for anyone in the room with her, she found herself alone.

After a few minutes Greyson walks in and nearly shouted her name in joy at seeing her awake. He ran over to her and kissed her forehead. "How are you feeling?"

She recoiled from his touch, ignoring his question. "How could you let that happen to me?" she cried as tears streamed down her face. The heart monitor beeped faster.

"What are you talking about, Evelyn? I couldn't help that you passed out," he replied, confusion on his face.

"And why do you think that happened?" she accused, eyes narrowing at him. "You left me there to suffocate while you walked away with *her*."

"What..." he trailed off, not sure what she was talking about. "You must have bumped your head pretty hard. Babe, don't you remember what happened?"

"Oh, I remember exactly what happened. You left me there to die as he buried me alive!"

Greyson looked horrified. "Do you really think I'd let something like that happen? No, babe, you passed out inside the house after you saw something in the bedroom. No one tried burying you alive."

Evelyn thought for a minute, trying to remember if what he was saying was true. All she could see when she closed her eyes was the maniacal face of the man who buried her. She opened her eyes and looked down at her clothes: a hospital gown; not too helpful in determining the truth. She sighed. She had no choice but to believe him. "I'm sorry," she uttered.

He kissed her forehead again, attributing her outburst to her head injury. "Now, how are you feeling?" he asked again.

"Like shit," she mumbled. "I'm groggy and everything feels heavy, but thankfully I'm not in pain. You said I hit my head?"

"Yeah. You said you saw the man from the bathroom again in our bedroom then you just fell over."

"Makes sense why I felt pain in my head, then."

"You said you were buried alive and mentioned 'her.' Who?" he sat down on the chair next to the bed.

Evelyn's face reddened slightly and began to recount her experience. Halfway through, a nurse walked in, seeming delighted that she was awake. The nurse checked her vitals, asked how she was feeling, and updated her on what the doctors said. Turns out she has a concussion, but luckily didn't injure herself further. Evelyn thanked the nurse as she walked away.

Turning back to Greyson, she finished her story. He sat in silence, looking at the floor, head resting on his folded hands. He had already talked to the doctor about Evelyn's episodes and her upcoming psychiatric appointment, but this was on a different level. Not sure how to handle this, he was contemplating telling the doctor about this new development when Evelyn's voice calling his name broke through his thoughts. "I'm sorry. I'm just thinking and honestly? I don't know what to think. But I do know that you need help. You need more help than I can give." He frowned at her expression, which had turned sour. "Don't look at me like that," he said softly. "I'm just worried about you. You've been going downhill for weeks and now look at you! You're in the hospital hooked up to wires, thinking I left you to die! Evelyn, look, I love you, but you've got to know in your heart that I'd never do something like that. I wouldn't sit there idly while someone hurt you and I especially wouldn't walk away with another woman."

"I know," she said quietly. "I don't know where any of that came from and I'm sorry I accused you. It just felt so real and then waking up here," she gestured vaguely, "I think it sent me over the edge. Oh, Greyson, I need help. Do you think they'll lock me up?" He looked her in the eyes and saw the fear behind them.

"No, there's no reason to do that. You aren't a danger to yourself or anyone else. Well, aside from breaking your leg and passing out, but there's no reason for them to commit you." He tried doing his best to soothe her.

She started crying again and put her head in her hands. Greyson got up and gently placed his arms around her. The doctor walked in at that moment. "Everything alright?" he asked, looking at the pair.

"No," Evelyn admitted, sniffling. Greyson released her and sat back down.

"That's no good. Let's see what we can do to fix that. I'm Doctor Norris. Can you tell me a little bit about what's been going on?" He pulled up a rolling chair and sat next to her.

Evelyn summarized what had been going on the past couple of weeks: the dreams, the waking up in places and not remembering how she got there, the people she had been seeing – though she left out the part about the people being the dead couple that resided in the house before them.

Doctor Norris nodded his head. "Was there a specific incident that brought this on? Any head injuries that you can remember?"

Evelyn bit her lip, not wanting to admit out loud what started all of this. "Well...the first nightmare happened the day we found out there had been two murders in our house before we bought it."

"Murders?" That piqued his curiosity.

"Alyssa and Dean Stanton in New Woogrea," Greyson explained. "Happened about two years ago."

The doctor stroked his chin, trying to recall the incident. "I think I remember that," he said. "That happened at your place?"

"Yeah," Greyson responded. "It's really shaken her up."

Looking at Evelyn, Doctor Norris commented, "Your husband mentioned you've got an appointment soon with a psychiatrist. Are you still planning on going?"

"Yes," she replied a little too quickly. "Definitely."

"I think that's the best course of action. I'll be honest, that's not my expertise, and I'd hate to tell you something that would be wrong or contradict what they will tell you."

"Appreciate your honesty," Greyson said genuinely.

"So, aside from that, you've got a concussion, which I'm sure your husband here or the nurse has already told you. My advice to you is to rest for about two days. Sleep is your friend; your brain needs to recover. You may have a headache for several days and you can take certain over the counter pain killers. I'll have those listed in your discharge paperwork. Can return to work – light duty – in three days, but listen to your body. If you don't feel like you can handle it, don't go. Any questions?"

"Just one. When am I getting discharged?" Evelyn asked.

"Shortly," he replied. Evelyn sighed in relief. They both thanked the doctor as he walked out of the door.

Two hours later, Evelyn was laying with her eyes closed on their couch with a bag of ice on her head. Greyson was busy preparing dinner in the kitchen. The scent of hamburgers would normally make her mouth water, but today the smell made her nauseated. She lightly groaned and put a throw pillow over her face.

Though she was in total control, the feeling of the weight over her face made her panic and she shot up, pillow and ice flying. Heart and head pounding, images of being buried flashed through her mind. She grit her teeth, telling herself that it wasn't real. She glanced around, eyes landing on the dark bedroom, door wide open. She thought she saw something move in the darkness. Her breath hitched as she stared, eyes wide, at the room.

Nothing happened.

Forcing her eyes shut, she lay back down. *There's nothing there,* she kept repeating to herself like a mantra. Peeking through one eye, she glanced towards the bedroom again. This time she definitely saw something.

"Greyson!" she shouted. She heard the clatter of the spatula against the griddle and his footsteps as he rushed over. She pointed towards the darkness. "In the bedroom!"

Not this again, he thought as he quickly walked to turn on the bedroom lights. After inspecting the place, he found nothing, just as he suspected. He came out of the bedroom shaking his head and shut the light off behind him.

Evelyn bit her lip and looked away. Greyson didn't say anything as he walked back to the kitchen, briefly stopping to kiss the top of her head. A few seconds later, she heard the scraping of the spatula and sizzling of the cooking meat. Looking off towards the bedroom again, she stared into the darkness.

This time she saw two dimly glowing eyes staring back at her. She stifled a scream and tried to convince herself it was just a hallucination, but she couldn't look away. It was as if she were trapped - like a deer in headlights.

The eyes bobbed up and down as if whatever was hiding in the darkness was walking towards her. Slowly the eyes inched closer, stopping just out of reach of the light.

Evelyn didn't realize she was holding her breath.

The eyes disappeared from view.

She frantically strained her eyes, willing herself to see into the darkness to find whatever that just was. Not daring to get up, she lay there, staring wide-eyed. There was a quick movement and in a flash, something was running towards her at inhuman speed. She didn't even have time to scream.

Chapter 34

Greyson stood at the stove searing onions on the griddle laid over the burners, oblivious to what was happening to his wife in the other room. The scent of cheese, burgers, and onions mingled in the air. He hummed a little as he cooked, trying to distract himself from the day's little adventure. The hospital is the last place he expected to be today, but when Evelyn collapsed in front of him, there was no question about what to do next.

When she didn't wake up for about a minute, he lifted her and quickly carried her to the car. He drove to the hospital as quickly as he could with a limp, unconscious wife in the front seat. Maybe he should have called an ambulance, but at the time he felt like he could get to the hospital quicker than an ambulance would be dispatched. He arrived in 12 minutes.

He tried to keep his cool at the hospital, knowing he would just be in the way as the doctors examined her and took her for testing. He impatiently sat in the waiting room, leg bouncing in anticipation, until they called him back.

He sat with her, talking to her until he talked his mouth dry and he needed a bottle of water. When he returned, he was elated to see she was awake. He wanted to run up to her and hug her, but realized how fragile she was. Plus, the look on her face made him hesitate.

Her accusations shocked him to the core. How could she, even in her state, believe he would ever do anything like that to her? And the other woman, where did that come from? Who was she? Did Evelyn have some insecurities he never picked up on?

He was lost in thought and didn't hear the footsteps over the cooking food. He felt a searing pain in his back and spun around to find Evelyn standing there, holding a now bloody knife. "Evelyn?" he gasped in horror, eyes bouncing from the knife to her blank face.

Faster than he could react, she raised the knife again and plunged it into his chest. He instinctively tried stepping backwards, only to be met with the stove. She lunged at him again, but this time he was faster, sidestepping out of her way just in time. Bleeding from two severe wounds, Greyson started breathing heavily. "What the fuck are you doing, Evelyn?!" he shouted, dodging her again.

She didn't answer, but the blank look on her face was replaced with hatred.

He tried grabbing her arms to stop her, but she overpowered him, slicing at his arm. "Evelyn! Stop!" Breathing now becoming labored, he staggered to the other side of the kitchen, reaching for his phone. With unnatural speed and strength, she shoved him, causing him to slip in his own blood and fall to the tile floor. He looked at her with fear and confusion in his eyes. "Why?" he gasped.

Wordlessly, she stepped over to him and placed her foot on the wound in his chest, pressing down. He sucked air in between his grit teeth and squirmed in pain. He tried shoving her off, but it was like trying to move stone. *What the fuck is going on?* he thought. She made a growling-like sound in her throat and stomped on his shoulder, dislocating it. He screamed.

She crouched down by his head, examining his facial expressions. Silently, she reached and slowly, shallowly slit his throat, wanting him to feel every inch of the incision, but not wanting to kill him…yet. He tried stopping her with his other arm, but she merely grabbed it with one hand and snapped the bone. He had tears streaming down his face in pain and his breathing was coming out in loud gasps.

His entire upper body in pain, he looked up at the woman he loved as she stared back at him, unfeeling, uncaring. Greyson felt like he was suffocating. He tried standing up, but with two useless arms, that proved almost impossible. Evelyn saw what he was trying to do and kicked him hard in the abdomen. Having the air knocked from him, he gasped again, trying futilely to catch his breath. He began coughing and felt blood coming from his mouth. *Fuck*.

He knew he wouldn't survive this. He saw her step over him, looking down at his face. He looked back up at her, tears in his eyes. He saw her raise the blade, slowly this time, then using all her strength she plunged the knife deep in his chest. "I love you," he whispered out before everything went black.

Chapter 35

Evelyn awoke on the kitchen floor with no recollection of how she got there. She felt wet and looked down at herself, her body and clothes stained red with blood. She screamed and looked around. Blood everywhere. Then she saw Greyson's body with the knife still lodged in his chest. She screamed again and scrambled over to him. "Greyson! Greyson!" She shook him, but his eyes wouldn't open. He was covered in blood with a gash across his throat.

She quickly reached out and grabbed his phone on the counter and dialed 911. She cried hysterically to the dispatcher, trying to explain the scene in front of her. The dispatcher tried to calm her down, letting her know that help was on the way. Evelyn didn't hear him.

She dropped the phone and threw herself over Greyson's lifeless body, sobbing inconsolably into his chest. Who could have done this? Why? Realization hit her as she stilled. The dispatcher was still trying to get her attention. She picked up the phone, still sniffling, voice thick with tears, and whispered, "I did it." She ended the call.

Knowing what she had to do, she stood up and moved robotically towards the bedroom. She didn't bother to turn on the lights, feeling her way through the dark. She reached Greyson's nightstand and reached inside the top drawer.

Feet padding against the floor, she mindlessly walked towards the kitchen. She got on her knees and crawled towards her husband's body. She leaned over him, kissed his bloodied lips, and whispered, "I love you." She closed her eyes and pulled the trigger.

Standing off to the side, a figure watched the couple. After a few minutes, it wordlessly faded away.

CHAPTER 36

It had been three months since Greyson woke up in the ICU. Three months since his world had shattered. Three months since he was left alone. Though he had friends and family come out of the woodworks to support him, without his wife by his side he felt utterly alone. People were constantly telling him how things were going to get better and how he was going to get past this, but he knew he would never recover.

Who were those people to tell him that? Had they ever been on the brink of death? Brutally attacked and left for dead by the one they loved? Had their loved one blow their brains out on their unconscious body? No, no one in his life had experienced the horrors he did. Sure, everyone had their own demons, but he was damned if he was going to let anyone tell him how he should be feeling and when he should be feeling it.

He sighed as he stared at the bare walls of his duplex. After what happened, he couldn't live in that house anymore. He didn't want any of the furniture, any of the appliances, any of the pots, pans, utensils, nothing. He wanted nothing to do with any of it.

Just the same as he did every evening, he started to relive his last moments with her. The blank stare on her face transitioning to a look of pure hatred. Where did that hatred come from? What had he done to her to cause such loathing? As far as he knew, they were a happy couple. Sure, they had their arguments, but nothing to ever cause such strong emotions like that.

He knew he was never going to get answers just as much as he knew he would never recover emotionally. Why had he survived? He didn't want to live in a world without her. Didn't want to live in this world after what she had done to him. He was in constant physical pain from the damage done, though it was nothing compared to the emotional pain – when he actually felt it. Most of the time he was numb.

For as much bad-mouthing his company as he had done in the past, they came through for him in the end. They were patient with him as he recovered, constantly reassuring him that he would not lose his job in addition to everything else he lost and they had kept their word. Though he told his boss several times he was quitting, his boss always talked him out of it. It's not that he didn't like the job or want the job, it was that he just didn't care about anything anymore.

He scowled. People talk about how near-death experiences cause them to appreciate life more. Well, the exact opposite had happened for him. Though he was going to a therapist and was on various mental health medications, he still wasn't right – and likely never would be.

He sighed and stood up, walking towards the bedroom. He flicked the light switch off and the room plunged into darkness. Not bothering with his hygiene, he lay on the bed. He knew sleep wasn't going to come easy, but then again, what was easy nowadays? Though he dreaded the nightmares that came every night, a small part of him welcomed them because that was the only time he got to see her. He let out a breath he didn't know he was holding and tightly shut his eyes, silently hoping, just like every night, this would be his last night alone and he could finally join Evelyn again.

Tonight's nightmare was different. She wasn't attacking him, oddly enough. Instead, he was trapped in his own body as he watched her being buried alive by a grotesque man. He tried to scream, to run towards her, to stop what was happening, but his body wouldn't obey. His head turned to the side as he glanced at the woman standing next to him. *Lexi?* He thought.

His body moved on its own as he walked towards the open grave to look at his wife's face. Greyson struggled against himself, trying to let go of Lexi and help Evelyn. Instead, he heard himself say "Finish the job; I'm tired of dealing with this," and he turned his back on his wife, wrapping his hand tighter around Lexi's waist. His heart broke as he heard his wife scream his name and out of the corner of his eye, he saw Lexi turn her head to look back at Evelyn, a smile on her face. Together, they walked away slowly.

Greyson awoke before his alarm, the echoes of his name on Evelyn's lips ringing in his ears. He had no desire to fall back asleep, so decided to get ready for work, despite it being 5 a.m. He slowly drove to work, not paying attention to the road.

Upon arriving, he made a beeline for the break room to brew a pot of coffee. An hour and a half later, other employees started to arrive. Greyson was busy typing away at his computer when he heard a soft knock. Entirely too focused on his work, he didn't notice Lexi had been watching him from his doorway for some time. He looked up and gruffly greeted her, not bothering to fake a smile. She took the opportunity to come into his office and stand behind him, hand resting on his shoulder.

"I'm not in the mood, Lexi," he warned her.

"Oh, you're never in the mood," she teased.

"I'm serious. Leave," he commanded.

She just waved him off and placed her hand on his back. "I think the proper greeting is 'Good morning.' Last I checked at least."

"Lexi," he warned again.

"Please, you know I'm just playing. You're far too serious. Look, I know you've been through hell, but that doesn't mean your life is over."

"Out. Now."

She ignored him and continued. "You need someone to keep you distracted and well...I'm great at distractions."

"This conversation is over. Get out of my office, now!"

She leaned in and whispered, hot breath caressing his ear, "You know you want to." She stood up straight and walked away, swaying her hips. Her eyes flashed as she twirled a silver and red pendant in her fingertips, a wicked smile on her face. She had planted the seed. Now to wait. She would get him. After all, she had nothing but time. He escaped once. This time, he wouldn't be so lucky.

Epilogue

Greyson stared at the TV in a daze as Lexi lay cuddled up next to him. She wasn't paying attention to the TV either, her mind on the man sitting next to her. She smiled as she ran her hand up his thigh. He ignored the advance, stood up, and walked over to the kitchen. *What are you doing with yourself, Greyson?* he thought. Evelyn's face flashed in his mind and he was suddenly disgusted with himself. He walked back to the living room, eyes landing on the woman sprawled out on the couch. "Lexi, I think you should go," he said.

She quickly sat up. "What's wrong? I thought we were having a good time?"

"I just can't do this," he sighed.

"Come on," she purred. "You said your neighbor isn't home. The place is all ours." She stood up and walked over to him.

He took a step back. "Lexi, please..."

She ignored him and placed her hand on his chest. "Just don't think, okay?" She reached up and gently kissed him.

He tightly shut his eyes and stepped back. "Look, I just can't. I'm going to use the restroom. Please go." He walked off as she stared after him, her expression darkening.

§

"What do you mean this happened before?" Detective Walsh asked.

"Remember the Stanton case in New Woogrea a couple years ago?" Sheriff Rowe gruffly responded.

"No, I don't. Not from here, remember?" Walsh replied.

"Well, picture this scene." Rowe gestured towards the body on the floor. "Except with two." Walsh's eyes slightly widened in surprise as he opened his mouth to comment, but Rowe continued. "The husband was found with burns all over his face and body and, well, it looked like he suffered before he died - several stab wounds, cut tendons likely so he couldn't escape, gashes across his back and arms. The murder weapon? A machete found next to his body."

"You said there were two?"

"Yeah. The second one – the wife – she was dead a while before him. Coroner said she was beaten and strangled. Only the husband's DNA was found on her – on her throat, under her fingernails, you get the gist. Another strange thing? She had no clothes on, but again, only the husband's DNA was found," he paused, "and only hers on him."

"What happened? Break-in gone wrong?"

"No signs of a break-in. Only thing was the lock on the bathroom door."

"Wait, they were found in the bathroom, too?"

"Yeah, are you paying attention?"

Walsh grit his teeth. "You didn't say that."

The sheriff ignored him and walked around the body. "Got a name?" he asked a deputy standing off to the side.

"Greyson Reed," he replied as he looked at the driver's license in the wallet he was holding. "Neighbor called it in. Davis is talking to him now." The sheriff walked over and caught part of the conversation.

"...didn't show up for poker night. Thought it was strange he didn't answer his phone or the door when I knocked. He always answered.

At first, I thought, hey, maybe he's out. But after a couple of days and no returned call, texts, or sight of him, I called for the wellness check."

"How long has it been since you've seen him?" Sheriff Rowe asked.

"Like I was telling this gentleman here, I was out of town visiting my grandchildren in Virginia, so it's been about a week and a half. I left on the 15th, came home on the 21st. Poker night was the 22nd and I hadn't seen him since before I left."

"Do you know of anyone who would have done this?"

The neighbor shook his head. "He was a quiet person who usually kept to himself. Didn't really have any visitors that I ever saw or heard." He looked down and sighed. "Can't believe this happened. He was such a good guy."

"Appreciate the information, sir," Rowe said as he turned to let Davis finish the conversation. He walked over to the bathroom to look at Greyson's body and just stared at it. It had been a while since he had seen something so gruesome. Laying crumpled in the bathtub, he had multiple wounds all over his body with blood soaked through his clothes. He was lying in a puddle of coagulated blood and there were splatters over the walls. But the worst part – his face was an angry red and blistered, as if he were burned with something. He sighed and shook his head, eyes passing over his hand lying limply at his side. Something shining caught his attention.

He narrowed his eyes and stepped closer to the tub. He pulled out a pen and with his gloved hand, pulled out what was grasped in Greyson's discolored hand.

It was a shining red and silver pendant.

§

Despite the oddly placed necklace in Greyson's hand, no DNA other than his was found in the apartment. There was no murder weapon, no footprints in the blood on the floor, no signs of a break-in, nothing. Another mystery, just like the Stanton case.

Throughout the investigation, despite the flashing cameras and wild theories thrown about, nobody saw the dark figuring hiding in the shadows – watching, waiting. Its presence nestled into the darkest corner of the room where the light didn't quite reach, remaining perfectly still with only the patience that the dead possessed. Dozens had entered, their focus sharp, however not a single eye turned towards the shadow that stretched a little too long.

After the last investigator left, the door closed for the last time, and the house returned to silence, the figured finally faded away.

www.ingramcontent.com/pod-product-compliance
Lightning Source LLC
Chambersburg PA
CBHW031036310726
48969CB00007B/2005